In the private room on th̶e̶ ̶.̶.̶.̶ on the edge of the bed, de̶l̶v̶e̶d̶ ̶i̶n̶t̶o̶ ̶h̶e̶r̶ ̶b̶a̶g̶ ̶f̶o̶r̶ ̶p̶a̶p̶e̶r̶ and pen, and began listing what she wanted Robin to bring from home when he returned later. He, having picked up some pinks from the downstairs flower shop, was looking for a vase. He was about to call the nurse when Gillian said abruptly, "Lock the door."

"What?" he asked.

"We got about fifteen minutes before anyone comes in," she said. "Just time for a quickie."

Robin's smile was painful. It has been more than two years since they had made love. He threw the flowers on the bed. "Sure, kid, get 'em off," he said. And made an exaggerated show of undoing his belt.

Gillian giggled. "There was a time," she said.

"Yes. There was a time," he replied. She tenderly touched his arm as he leaned over and kissed her forehead.

...the fifteenth floor, Gillian sat
...fed into her bag for paper

& Gillian

Alvin Rakoff

WARNER BOOKS

A *Warner* Book

First published in in Great Britain in 1996
by Little, Brown and Company
This edition published in 1996 by Warner Books

A CIP catalogue record for this book
is available from the British Library.

ISBN 0 7515 1764 X

Typeset by Palimpsest Book Production Limited
Printed in England by Clays Ltd, St Ives plc

UK companies, institutions and other organisations wishing
to make bulk purchases of this or any other book
published by Little, Brown should contact their local
bookshop or the special sales department at the address below.
Tel 0171 911 8000. Fax 0171 911 8100.

Warner Books
A Division of
Little, Brown and Company (UK)
Brettenham House
Lancaster Place
London WC2E 7EN

To Jackie

Ampersand. It starts as Robin and Gillian. And becomes Robin & Gillian. On cards at Christmas for instance. Or invitations. Can Robin & Gillian make dinner on the 17th? In the minds of others. Linked. Robin & Gillian. What are Robin & Gillian doing? Where are Robin & Gillian going? What do Robin & Gillian think? Without separation, together, as one. Robin & Gillian. A unit.

The ampersand partner is usually female. Not always, but usually. Robin & Gillian. Richard & Annie. Hugh & Rohan. Sometimes it's Penny & Derek, or Barbara & Dickie, but not often. The male name usually leads. Not because of dominance. Or personality. More to do with custom. And sound. One name more readily following another. Sounds good. Sounds right. Even when the names are Malcolm & Carlo, Geoffrey & Alan, Molly & Lillian. Joined. Wedded by ampersand. And that whom ampersand hath joined together cannot easily be put asunder.

Ampersand. &. A symbol. A means of linkage. Short. Efficient. Convenient.

The ampersand partner. Following behind the name of the first. A trailer behind another vehicle, an ampersand the towbar. Second part of a twosome. Last half.

I

The other one in a double act, performing on all sorts of stages. The follower.

But can the first name exist without the ampersand and the second name?

Name plus ampersand plus name equals a relationship.

A name without an ampersand behind it and then another name means solitude.

Ampersand plus name is a story.

CHAPTER

I

Idiot! Idiot. Idiot. Idiot. IDIOT! He stood shouting at himself in the mirror unable to believe what he had done, or rather, what he had not done. Asshole! Asshole. Asshole. Asshole. ASSHOLE!! He roared. *Répétez après-moi en français*, as in school, *imbecile*. Or, *stupido! cretino!* What other languages should I use? he wondered. What other words are fit for self-insulting?

Cunt. No. That was not a word he liked to use except in passion. Sacred rather than profane.

Robin sighed, stared again at the mirror. He was aware of the growing wrinkles criss-crossing his face. Age, damn it, will soon stop you. You didn't have to stop yourself. He sighed again. How could I do nothing, how could I be such a fool? How could I have a woman as wantable as that in bed beside me all night and do nothing?

3

Another long look at the image in the looking glass. Then as punishment, he slapped himself, hard, across the face. And smiled. Not hard enough, he mused. Thoughts of his father made the smile leave his face. Blood splattered on the brown and cream checked linoleum of the family's kitchen floor. His father's blood. With clenched fist his father had stood in the centre of the kitchen repeatedly clubbing himself across his nose, his eyes, his mouth, his cheeks, his ears. "Dad, don't," pleaded a fifteen-year-old Robin. His father ignored him, not satisfied until more blood poured out of the lean, elegant face. Blood-letting. A regular event, about twice a year for as many years as Robin could remember. What caused it? Something the older Robin should have done and didn't? Or something he did do? Guilt or remorse? Robin never knew his father well enough to learn the answers. But on that day he had seen his baby sisters, as usual, run screaming from the room as the self-beating began. And Robin decided this tyranny of terror had to stop. He waited until the hand-hammer returned listlessly to his father's side and the old man leaned heavily, bleeding, against the back of a chair. He approached his father and said quietly, "If you ever do that again, I'll call the police." His father stared at him through blinking eyes like a drunk who, once sober, can never understand any accusations of drunkenness. Robin often wondered what he would have done had his father struck him.

4

Would he have hit back? His father was physically larger than he was. Stronger. But more important, he was Dad. Father. Robin senior. Could he strike his father? Fortunately he wasn't tested. The old man seemed purged, drained, exhausted of any need for more violence. As Robin silently watched, his father turned and went out onto the heavily screened porch ignoring his two young daughters still cowering in a corner behind chintz chairs. In the kitchen Robin mopped up the blood.

It never happened again.

Robin left the bathroom with its accusing mirror. And flopped into one of the easy chairs Gillian, his wife, had insisted be moved up from the living room to their bedroom to increase the cosiness, the comfort she needed while recuperating. He was still wearing pyjama bottoms. He didn't want to get dressed. No energy. Listless. Lifeless. Useless. Drained. It was over a week since it happened, since he met Clara. And he couldn't stop thinking about her, couldn't stop thinking about that night, couldn't stop hurling hurting words at himself, couldn't stop cursing himself, couldn't stop sighing. More than a week. I've got to stop, he told himself. More than a week and I know I can't stop.

Why didn't I fuck her? Why? Why? To spend all night with a woman in bed and not make love to her. Why?

And what a woman. Perfect. Well, almost perfect. Blonde. Slim. Small ass. Smooth skin. Small tits but what the hell. And her eyes were too close. But to me, almost perfect, thought Robin, recalling a happy glowing face.

"My name is Clara," she said. They were in the back of a taxi on the Periphery coming from Charles de Gaulle airport. She extended her hand. "Clara Stromehl."

So formal, he hid his amusement from her, so young. Her youth clouded her with an aura of innocence. And it was infectious. Robin felt almost giddy with flirtatiousness. She must be, what, one, maybe two – it couldn't be three, could it? – decades younger than me.

"I'm Robin." He took her hand, debated about lying about his last name in case events escalated to the plateau his mind had already reached. Take a chance, "Robin Laurent."

She settled back, slight apprehension showing in the rigidity of her body.

"I don't know any 'Robins'," she said after a while.

"I don't know any 'Claras'," said Robin. "Y'see, we have so much in common."

She smiled.

"And where are you from, Clara Stro–om–?"

She spelled out her name slowly, deliberately, a rote

she was apparently used to performing. Robin listened. But was more aware of painted lips forming each letter than of sounds made. "I'm from California," she said finally.

"And where in California?"

"San Diego," she replied. "And you?"

"Born in Paterson, New Jersey," he said. "Been living in London for the past fourteen years."

"London, hmm. That must be nice, to live there I mean. Is it?" she asked.

"Well, let's say it beats Paterson, New Jersey."

She nodded. "Does it beat New York?" she asked, then added quickly, "I like New York."

"So do I. So did I. I like them both," he said. She looked at him, wanting more. "I've lived and worked in both cities." He paused. "It's easier to work in New York. Easier to live in London." Another pause, while he reconsidered, then said, "Or maybe it's the other way round."

For the first time Clara laughed. A wholesome laugh. She turned to look out of the window while his eyes detailed her face. She must have been aware of his staring.

After a while she turned back.

"What brings you to Paris on a Saturday night in July?" she asked.

"Conference. Pre-conference tomorrow. Proper conference Monday." Obviously sounded boring enough to her, he thought, she's not asking any more questions.

The images flashed over the taxi windows, images of black and white melding into grey, melding into the nothingness of suburban routes from airport to city. Robin didn't feel the need to make conversation. He felt relaxed. Delighted. Delighted not only to be with this refreshing young woman. But delighted with her for her own sake for being so young, so amiable, so handsome.

"Will you barbecue the roast or shall I do it in the oven?" Gillian's shout up the stairs broke today into last week. "When are you coming down? Are you dressed?" And then added, "The boys will be back soon. Famished. You curse when it doesn't light."

"I don't curse," Robin shouted back. Except at my image in a mirror, he said to himself.

"Yes, you do swear," said Gillian, "all that Shi-ite Muslims and Focker-Wolfe. The way you drawl it out. 'Oh, shiiiii-iiiiite!' and 'Fockerrrrr-Wolfe it!' Substituting. Doesn't fool anyone. Not even Vanessa."

Aunt Vanessa, the childless vicar's widow from Newcastle, wife of Gillian's late brother, had taken their two sons ice skating.

"Barbecues don't light in this country," said Robin. "Not the way they do back home."

"Speak to Baroness Thatcher," said Gillian.

"D'y'think the neighbours are enjoying this conversation?" asked Robin. The windows were wide open.

"More than I am, I'm sure," said Gillian. "Besides, if you're not down in fifteen minutes, I'm throwing the roast over the Wallace fence." She raised her voice. "This is an advance warning. A leg of lamb is about to hit you, dear Wallaces. Scots wha' hae! Take cover."

Despite himself, Robin chortled. He could hear the handstick she recently needed, tapping away from the stairwell. He started to dress.

Robin wondered, how accurate is memory? In a week am I already falsifying, romanticizing the incidents? No, I don't think so.

Gillian, as always, drove him to Heathrow. Since April, when the disease had relented its crippling grip and most of her energy had returned, she rejoiced in performing mundane wifely chores. Driving her husband to the airport was one of those chores. The peck on the cheek, the words "have a good time" issued almost as an order, certainly an instruction, then waiting in the car until the final salute just before the parting doors of the terminal building take him away. An easy scene. Husband and wife at an airport. He departs while she drives home. Domestic. Marital. Routine. Part of a pattern.

At the gate he first saw the girl who was later to introduce herself as Clara. It was a measuring glance. That's all he allowed himself these days. He had long passed the stage and age of believing he still registered with young women, knowing they were looking past him, focusing consciously and unconsciously on unwrinkled, more prowling males.

"Isn't it awful, now you walk into a room — any room, boardroom, restaurant, meeting place — and they don't look you in the eyes. Isn't it shitty?" Peter, his partner, was speaking over coffee after a dinner at Rules. "The coiffeured heads no longer turn towards you."

Peter was, as usual, immaculate. Dressed in regulation blue pinstripe, complementary shirt, subtle tie, a discreet but definite showing of goldwear on wrists and cuffs, he sat back to light a cigarette. Once-blond hair, still full, outlined a classically handsome English face. He was, like Robin, well into middle age. Peter would not let go of the subject. In one's youth girls surveyed you for physical appearance, he insisted, later for what you could do to help their careers. "Then finally, you wake up one morning transformed. You haven't done a thing. Not a thing. But you've changed. Completely." Peter exhaled. "The ladies with the made-up eyes look right through you. I want to grab a fistful of that highlit hair and shout, 'Look, it's me! Me! I'm still here.'" Peter snorted. "But it's like The Man said, last stage of all," he was gently easing into an obvious quote, but wasn't quite sure even if after all these years his alien partner would know it, "sans everything!"

"Are you trying to tell me it's not 'As You Like It'?" said Robin.

Both men laughed.

The crowd at the gate herded forward, handing over boarding-cards to a besieged desk, as if fearful that designated seats were bound to be usurped by unknown interlopers. Robin, who hated surging masses, decided to buy a newspaper. At a shop nearby he found the only readable paper left was *The Times*. He returned to join a reduced line-up at the gate. And that was when he first saw Clara.

She was dressed in white. With tanned face, well-tended flashes of sun-shaded hair, slim body, he was certain that his were not the only pair of male eyes appraising her as she came forward. Other women in the crowd were just as pretty in varying ways as Clara. Look, that one. No, not her. Though she's not bad either. The brunette. Rounded high cheeks, tall, elegant. Friendly eyes. Considerably prettier. But Robin's eyes returned to Clara. None of the others was as distinctive to him as the young lady in white.

Clara joined the queue slowly, almost reluctantly, all the while wheeling her hand luggage on a carry-on trolley. Her movements were innocently sensuous. A man with linebacker shoulders forced his way past Robin and others, leaned forward, spoke to her. Robin watched. She did not reply. After a while the linebacker stopped, the burly shoulders drooping perceptibly.

Whether at this point she was aware of Robin or not he would never know.

On board, he saw her being directed to the front of the plane while he sat two cabins further back. And thought no more about her.

The flight itself was the way Robin preferred such trips to be in these days of hijack and terrorism. Boring. Except for a class of Japanese schoolgirls, a sort of oriental St Trinian's seated all around him, speaking French at a terrifying speed, determined to practise their impressive mastery of a foreign tongue as if the flight were a crammer course before a final examination to occur soon after landing. They giggled, screamed polysyllabic words in singsong voices at each other and at anyone else available. The French vocabulary of a well-trained but definitely-not-fluent British stewardess was soon exhausted. They then turned to the other passengers. Including Robin. He hid behind the

12

broadsheets of *The Times*. It worked. For the first time Robin acknowledged a debt to Rupert Murdoch.

At French passport control Clara approached the queue at a right-angle, revealing her ignorance of the disciplined lines the British form while waiting. Where's she from? Robin wondered. French? Maybe. Scandinavian? Don't think so. Robin contrived, by faltering a bit, to arrive at the point where the line of her approach intersected his. Should I start? What the hell. Why not. *Courage, mon brave.* Speak. See what happens.

"Can I put my bag on your trolley?" he asked her.

"What? I'm sorry, I can't hear what—"

Her accent was the same as his. "My bag, my case, can I put it on your trolley?"

She smiled. With the noise of the airport and his nervous garbling of the words, she obviously had difficulty hearing him. Or is trolley called cart in the States? Damn, I can't remember, Robin said to himself.

"Yes, wheels are useful," she replied, confirming she hadn't completely heard his question.

Robin held back, semi-indicating that she could join the line in front of him. She pretended not to notice and filed in somewhere behind him.

The carousel handling the flight's luggage was not clearly marked. She'll have trouble. Bet on it. He questioned himself. Should I double back? Damsel in distress. Prince, well, knight at least, to the rescue. Well okay, frog to the rescue. But even frogs like being kissed.

13

Too bloody corny. The agency would never allow that as a premise. For such thoughts, dear Robin, you could be banish-ed – Shakespearean pronunciation, please – to the Gruber & Franklin agency in Newark where you began a quarter of a century ago. No chance. Look at her. White sandals, edged in natural leather beige; white trousers, probably silk; the top gave one the illusion of being able to see through broad-stitched gaps, but it was only an illusion; it was well cut, sloping down to white tassels hanging provocatively over her front and bum. Stylish. The lady has money and youth and looks. And she doesn't need you, Robin. No chance. No chance at all. Anyway, you were never any good at picking up women, never had the smarm and the words. Never ever. Only had the looks. But too damn shy. Better settle for a quiet night cuddling up to an inviting glass of malt whisky.

Clara was putting her passport into her shoulder bag – also white, also piped in beige leather – scouring the electric signboards. Her eyes had already taken on the bewildered look of the traveller.

"Do you know where our luggage is?" It was Robin who did the asking. Better to be the questioner rather than wait, and hope, to be questioned. A forward step. Almost aggressive. Not a bad ploy. Not bad.

"It says number four." She pointed to a bilingual neon indicator.

"No. That's the gangway they want us to exit from. For Customs," he said. 'There it is."

Behind her the carousel numbers clacked round. They walked back together, agreeing the signs in English and French were too many and too confusing. And waited for the bags to trundle round.

"I have to get to Orly airport," she said.

"That's the other side of Paris." He was surprised.

"Yes, I know," she said.

"Buses are out there. But I'm taking a taxi into town, the ninth arrondissement," he said. "You're welcome to share it." She hesitated. "Easier to get a train or taxi from town," he added.

"Thanks," she replied, "but ..." he waited for the turndown "... only if I can pay for my half."

"There's no need to do that."

Her two suitcases, both heavy and large, finally arrived. She insisted he load them onto her already overcrowded trolley rather than search for an airport cart.

"Let's go," he said.

"What about yours?"

"I don't have any. Only staying two nights. Just this – " Robin lifted his overnight case.

"I see."

She hesitated. Now she must realize he could have left the airport long before she did. That she was his reason for delaying. Crunch time. Will she stay or will she come along? Without turning to see if she was behind him, he led the way towards the taxis. He was half-convinced,

15

apprehensive if not fearful, she might not follow. But after a beat, she did.

The chattering taxi drivers argued vehemently as to who was to be their chauffeur until finally they were settled in front of a happy little Asian, either Vietnamese or Korean, who spoke little French and who tried to make up for it by a perpetual grin. Robin carefully gave him the name of the hotel, the address, the arrondissement or district, and told him it was near the Folies-Bergère. And settled back in the taxi.

That's when she had introduced herself as Clara Stromehl.

The greyness of the world outside the taxi continued endlessly.

"You're a very pretty girl, Clara Stromehl."

"Don't," she said firmly. "You don't have to say that."

"I know I don't." Robin wondered if he dared link his little finger round hers. He dared. He slid his hand across the seat. "But I like telling the truth."

"Thank you," she said and took her hand away.

"But you're right, I shouldn't have said you're a very pretty girl. Dr Kingston would never forgive me." She looked at him. "Dr Kingston of Paterson High. He always said 'Try not to use the word "very" when writing or speaking or even thinking. It's a nothing word.' Sorry, Dr Kingston." He paused. "Don't you like compliments?"

She did not answer but turned away to look out of the car's window. She was pretty. Not beautiful. Certainly not as beautiful as Gillian had been at the same age. Nor had she the relentless beauty of a model. At work he was surrounded by models, the "glamorous but not amorous" Peter called them. Cold, ambitious, unapproachable and often unlikeable. Both men had had their share of encounters with the sculpted mannequins. And no longer pursued "the skinnies and thinnies". Don't touch me there, could leave a bruise! Stop, not so many, my lips swell! Spanking? How dare you! Clara's looks were softer, more likeable, more durable, and more ordinary. An honest-faced, hearty girl, probably with a simple if not naive — especially so after his years in Europe — mentality.

"I lived in Paris," she said, as if to contradict his thoughts, "for a year. As a student. At the American University." She looked him full in the face for the first time.

"Oh! I know where that is," he said. "Used to watch students pour across the Pont de l'Alma. I had a flat near there, near Rue Marbeuf; I was working here for a few months. Always looked like they were enjoying themselves, those students."

"When was that?"

"About four years ago," he said.

"I was here six years ago. I did have a good time. But y'know what I remember most? The cold. I couldn't get warm." She giggled.

"Then you speak French?" he asked.

"Understood every word you've said so far," she smiled, "but I'm not as brave as you at trying it on."

"Why?" he asked, "why come here to study?" And regretted it. Don't answer. You'll become real. A girl. A woman. If this day is to end as I want it to end then just be a thing. You are just a thing. An object for loving. What the sisters say you shouldn't just be, for me please be. My wife is ill. I haven't made love to anything except my hands for two years. No, don't tell me who you are. I want to fuck you, not get to know you.

"Paris is Paris," she said. "If you're from Des Moines or Madison or even San Diego, and can get to study here for a year, you take it. Paris is Paris."

"A very Gertrude Stein sort of answer," he said.

"You've just used the word 'very' again," she said rather smugly. And sat back to indicate she would not, for the moment, reveal any more of herself.

Not for the first time the taxi driver was wrestling with a book, flicking pages back and forth, reading, his eyes darting repeatedly from page to road and back again while he drove well over the speed limit on the sardine-crowded motorway. In common with most Paris cabbies he did not know his way around anything other than the better known landmarks of the city. Numerous consultations with his book of street maps were therefore necessary. Turning pages with one hand, the driver's other hand rested, too nonchalantly for Robin's liking, on the steering wheel, except when it was used to dipsy the car recklessly from one lane to another, jamming his vehicle with frightening precision between other fast-moving cars. In the rear-view mirror Robin finally managed to catch the driver's eye. The grin on the cabby's face widened. Robin was not reassured. Nor were the continual brakings and then lurching accelerations much comfort to him. *"L'addresse, c'est difficile?"* asked Robin. Wider still and wider grew the grin on the driver's face. Robin repeated, loudly, the hotel's address, 106 Rue de Montyon. The driver turned his back on the motorway, faced Robin, still grinning. There were five Montyons in the book, which one would Robin like? The rear of the car in front loomed large in the windscreen and was about to enter the taxi when the driver managed to brake. Robin flipped through the pages.

For the first time Clara moved close to him. He could smell her. Her perfume, her body, her womanness, a feast of smells for his starving senses. He concentrated on the maps, debated about putting on glasses, then handed the book to Clara, saying her young eyes would find it quickly. She did. With a finger carefully placed on the open page, she leaned forward to show the driver. The outline of her back from curled tresses down past the slim, arched waist, finishing on rounded buttocks, tempted his yearning thoughts. And wishes.

"*Ah, oui,*" said the driver, "*c'est le neuvième, tout près de la Folies-Bergère.*"

"Didn't I say that?" Robin demanded of Clara. 'The ninth arrondissement, near the Folies.' Didn't I say that?"

"You did, you did," she laughed, "and in impeccable French."

"Ah, so that's what was wrong with it," he said.

CHAPTER

2

The taxi left the Periphery and began to needle its way through narrow streets, passing bars, bistros and restaurants already thronging with Saturday evening activity.

"Where are you going to stay near Orly?" Robin asked.

"I'll find a hotel." She nodded towards the front of the car. "I would ask the driver. But I don't trust 'em. You wind up at some second-cousin's place. And regret it."

"The concierge at my hotel," Robin suggested, "should be able to recommend a place."

A beat, then Clara nodded, "Yes. Good." She bit her lip. "Then I'll leave you."

"And you can have a meal on your own," said Robin, "and so can I. What's the sense in that? Two lonely eaters in the City of Light. At least wait till after dinner."

"I want to pay my share," she said.

"No," he said sharply, "you have to pay for both of us!" She was startled. Until he smiled. "I pay for dinner," he said.

Stopping at traffic lights, they gazed at pedestrians, most of them young, swarming past the taxi. The joyousness of the people and places of Paris began to infect Robin. When's the last time I was here? Two, no, damn, three years ago September. Too long. Too long away from a city that softens the soul. He wondered if it was having any effect on Clara.

"Maybe I can get a room at your hotel," she said abruptly.

Robin nodded. And added, "Or maybe I can change to a larger room. For the two of us." She looked at him but said nothing. "Aren't you going to protest?" he asked. "You wanted to pay for half the taxi, half the dinner, why not half the room?"

She shook her head. "Because it isn't going to happen," she said.

"*Voilà la Folies-Bergère!*" said the elated driver as if he had just at that moment finished creating the building.

The hotel was one of those long thin town houses on a street of long thin town houses all of which had been converted by entrepreneurial landlords a century ago. At the desk, the concierge was so young Robin suspected she was the member of the family who had drawn the short straw to work this Saturday night. He knew his room would not be lavish. Accommodation, paid for by the French secretariat, for a convention of graphic designers would not be overflowing with luxuries. Often in the past he had simply changed rooms. Or hotels. But Peter and the accounts office had recently chastized him for setting a bad example.

The plump teenager behind the desk was puzzled as she sifted through the reservation cards. "It is a room just for you, m'sieur," she stated, trying hard to be sophisticated and not glance too often at Clara.

"Do you have another room available?" he asked. To hell with Peter and the accountant.

"I regret," the concierge replied, "the hotel is complete. Full. The last Saturday in July, before the August holidays, Paris is busy."

"Paris is always busy," Robin said. And looked at Clara. "What about changing, a larger room? For two?"

"Nothing, absolutely nothing," said the concierge, studying the lists, "I regret ..." Not nearly as much as I do, Robin thought.

"Let's check the room out," he suggested, "have a drink and then find some place for dinner. Then a hotel for you."

Clara, who had stood silently by throughout this

exchange, manoeuvred her cart into the deserted hotel bar adjacent to the front desk. She made sure the luggage was hidden from public view, but where the concierge could easily keep watch. To Robin's surprise the hotel had an elevator. They squeezed in. And the elevator, creaking and cranking, made its lethargic way to the eighth floor.

He opened the door to one of the beige-filled hotel rooms of the world. Featureless, characterless, and small. "There is a school of designers going around creating non-memorable hotel rooms," Robin said. Clara giggled. "Let's open the window," she suggested. She moved to do so and the late afternoon sun backlit her slim young figure.

"Y'know the best thing about this room?"

"This window?" she asked, struggling to open it.

"No, that's the second best thing." He was beside her, undoing the latch.

"What's the first?" Light and air entered the room.

"You," he said.

They stood at the window. After a beat, she responded. "Don't, please don't ... It isn't ... necessary. To talk like that. It makes me feel ... I want to be your friend. Not your ..." She couldn't finish.

How many nights does it take to know a woman? A hundred? Ten? A thousand? How many nights are in a marriage? Ten years is three thousand six hundred and fifty nights. Forgetting leap years. So you are not going

24

to know this woman in one night. Her wants, her needs, her temper, her humour, her strength, her tears and all other of her 'hers' will not be revealed to you tonight, m'sieur. Anyway, the first night doesn't count. Nor the second. Maybe the first ten dozen nights don't count. A sampler period. Try-out time. Take it home and try it before you buy it. Alterations made to fit. Satisfaction guaranteed ... Stop it, stop it. But look at her. Pretty, young, healthy, desirable, perhaps even lovable. You just want to get her into bed, not into your head. Remember that. Just that. Nothing else.

"I'm just saying, I'm glad you're here," was all he said.

She turned away from Robin to prod the chair. Decided to chance it. "It'll do, as a room, for you, alone, won't it?"

The room did have all the necessary prerequisites. A bed. Robin wasn't sure if in New Jersey it would be called a three-quarter or a large single. Also present was a writing table. A television set. And a refrigerator-bar supposedly stacked with goodies such as booze and bottled water but for which the key — "*Je regrette, m'sieur*" — did not fit and so its contents remained forever inaccessible. And the chair, on which Clara could not hide her discomfort as she shifted from position to position. The adjoining bathroom was, again, tiny, though complete. A half-size tub with hand-held shower. A loo. A basin. With mirror. And, *quelle surprise*, a hair dryer.

"It's all right, but it won't be the same when you go." Robin glanced outside. Maybe it was the ordinariness of the rooms that made the windows in Parisian hotels stand out, elegant French windows that spanned from ceiling to floor but only led onto a ridiculously small balcony no deeper than two feet. Beyond which the grey-green leaded roofs of the city stretched endlessly to the horizon.

On the street below young men, barely out of their teens, revved up motorbikes of varying sizes. Girlfriends watched. All shouted at each other above the noise of the cycles. It was not going to be a quiet night.

A knock on the door signalled the arrival, handed over by a sullen cleaning lady, of a bottle of warm Perrier and a few miserable slips of ice.

"All I have is Scotch," Robin said.

She nodded. "Not too much for me."

The chair was abandoned. Clara rose, tapped the bed, sat down, and tucked her legs under her. "How much is this room?" she asked.

"About two hundred, two hundred and twenty-five dollars."

"Gawd, think of what you could get for that in California," she said.

"Now tell me the story of your life." He gave her the drink.

"You first," she said.

"My life started when I met you," he said.

"Are you married?" she asked.

Direct. Right on the button. Lady wants to know the answer before proceeding further. "I am married," he said.

"No ring on your finger."

"I hate jewellery," he said. "And I hate the idea. Tied to someone by eighteen kays of gold."

"Doesn't your wife mind?" she asked. "You not wearing a ring?"

Robin had to pause for a moment. "I never asked her," he said. He sipped his drink. Warm. The ice long melted. "My wife is sick. Very sick. Damn. There I go again, the word 'very'. That's why she's not with me. And you?"

"I'm on my way to Malaga," she said. "That's in Spain."

Robin choked on the drink, laughing. "I don't think we're in Kansas any more, Toto ..."

Clara was puzzled.

"Wizard of Oz. Judy to the dog."

Clara smiled. "Of course," she said. "Tired. Sorry. Didn't sleep much last night. On the plane. Or the night before."

"I know where Malaga is. So does three-quarters of Europe. It'll be crowded." He sipped again. "Meeting him there, are you?"

She was not unaware of the question's phrasing. "Her," she said. "My girlfriend's already there. This year we wanted somewhere different."

"It'll be different. Not like San Diego, not an inch of space on the sands of Malaga. I don't know why anybody from the West Coast comes here. Your beaches are better, bigger, wider, cleaner. Must be the bad-tempered waiters sniggering behind your backs. Or the diarrhoea, the dirty sea, the huge mosquitoes, and let's not forget the no-air-conditioning . . ." He could see her face drop. "But you'll have a great time!" Robin laughed. And Clara laughed.

"Ready for dinner?" asked Robin. Clara nodded. He finished his drink. Took her hand to help her off the bed. And they left.

CHAPTER

3

The hospital waiting room was crowded with fellow sufferers. Help me. Save me. Don't let me die. Let him die. Not me. Take my disease away. Burn it. Wash it. Cut it out of me. It's in me. In me. Me. Me. Me. Get it out. Out. Out. Out. Unspoken torments seen in the eyes of others.

But not in Gillian's eyes. Gillian knew she was not going to die. Knew it. Believed it. Knew it. She would conquer this scourge. With radiotherapy and chemotherapy, with medication and meditation, with pills and potions, bottles and books, conventional medicine and alternative medicine, Chinese herbs and old-fashioned crystals, vitamins and voodoo, with a mixture of all things practical and the right things spiritual, she would not die. It would not kill her. Kill others maybe. But not her. She knew it.

Robin sat beside Gillian on the torn, uncomfortable, hospital-green vinyl benches. The routine was always the same. With three or more papers – usually *The Times*, the *Guardian*, *Telegraph* and the *Independent* – he could get through these mornings. The appointments were supposedly private. Timed. Dated. Official. But the same arrangements applied to National Health patients. And no differentiation was made between those asking the government to pay and those reaching into their own wallets. So the appointments were usually an hour off schedule. Probably fair enough, thought Robin. Democracy in this land of the first elected parliament was different. But why call it private when it isn't private? Why make an appointment that can never be kept on time? If I lived here another twenty decades, he thought, I still won't get it.

A nurse came forward, fat and jolly and Jamaican, to collect Gillian. All the nurses knew Gillian. Her serenity and strength and wit were notable. She was never depressed or down. Not in front of the nurses. Not in front of the doctors. Not often, thought Robin, in front of me. Not often.

The folds of flesh wobbled under the nurse's uniform as she walked down the corridor leading Gillian towards blood tests, urine tests, weight checks. Robin watched their retreating backs, jabbering away to each other, pretending to be oblivious that they would soon be measuring a disease's progress. Look at them. Fat and Skinny. The Laurel and Hardy of Charing Cross Hospital. Come and see the picture show, folks, the real live moo'm picture show. Price of admission? Only a dime, ten cents. Or one wife with cancer. Gillian had lost almost a third of her body weight in less than a year. And with the horror eating into her skeletal frame, she had also lost nearly a foot in height. Round-shouldered, stooped, almost a deformed back. "Look at me," she once shouted in front of the mirror, "I could be Charles Laughton in the fuckin' *Hunchback of Notre Dame*." He had waited for her to break. Saw her steel herself. No break. She left the room with dignity. That night in bed she said: "Poor Robin, who loves beauty so much, who sat in front of the David in Florence for hours and hours until the attendant threatened to call the police — '*pazzo inglese*', he called you, remember? — poor Robin is now stuck with me. Not a Michelangelo, am I? Just an ugly midget." He took her in his arms. Tried to speak. Tried to mouth some cliché of comfort. Her fingers covered his lips. "Don't," she said. He nodded. He brought her frail, bird-like form closer to him. And he began to cry. I cry, he thought, and she doesn't. I know who's the braver, the stronger. I must tell her. Talk to her. But he could say nothing. The tears melted down his cheek. Onto hers. Until they fell asleep.

✻   ✻   ✻

"Her blood count is low," said Professor Knights, "so I want to keep her in overnight. Blood transfusion."

The professor appeared to Robin more of an age to be a cricket-playing schoolboy than a medical specialist. Never mind policemen, when medical specialists start looking young, then you're really getting old.

"I've spoken to the fifteenth floor," said Knights, "they're expecting you."

Bedside charm was not the professor's strong point. He seemed to hope that an air of bluff scientific detachment might add years to his personality.

Gillian rose.

"Do I need three pints again?" she asked.

"You do," confirmed Knights.

"If we start now, I could be through by one or two in the morning," said Gillian. "I could go home then."

"If you insist," sighed Knights. He did not argue. He knew that the likelihood of Gillian having enough energy to leave hospital at that hour was remote. But it was a sort of game they had both fallen into. Because it was important to Gillian to be able to assert that she still had some control over her body, and over what others, including medical professors, could make her do.

Gillian smiled. And the professor, as always, gave the impression that he was quite relieved to see her and her husband go.

*   *   *

32

In the private room on the fifteenth floor, Gillian sat on the edge of the bed, delved into her bag for paper and pen, and began listing what she wanted Robin to bring from home when he returned later. He, having picked up some pinks from the downstairs flower shop, was looking for a vase. He was about to call the nurse when Gillian said abruptly, "Lock the door."

"What?" he asked.

"We got about fifteen minutes before anyone comes in," she said. "Just time for a quickie."

Robin's smile was painful. It had been more than two years since they had made love. He threw the flowers on the bed. "Sure, kid, get 'em off," he said. And made an exaggerated show of undoing his belt.

Gillian giggled. "There was a time," she said.

"Yes. There was a time," he replied. She tenderly touched his arm as he leaned over and kissed her forehead.

In a car, scouring estate agent's brochures, Gillian and Robin sat one rain-lashed evening looking at a house in West London. The need to find a building to store his family had become desperate enough for them to keep searching even on such a dismal night.

"Doesn't make sense," Robin said, "where are all these rooms? Must be in the back." He repeatedly checked the estate agent's photos and papers in Gillian's hands.

"Shall we go and look?" she asked.

"Why bother? Look at it. Pipes and drains and gutters. On the front of a house. Yuk."

"That window, the bay, that's nice," she said.

Minutes later they were standing in a living room the size of a minor ballroom. With windows on all four sides. Some high and out of reach. On another wall French windows led to a garden. And on a third wall a recess of windows, leaded and partially stained, featured strongly.

Gillian's eyes approved.

"I likee," she whispered to her husband.

"Me too," replied a subdued Robin. "Lots."

Upstairs in the artist's studio with its huge north-facing window, lofty beamed ceiling and galleried area, Gillian nodded at Robin. He smiled back. "Your den?" she suggested. "With a billiard table, as you've always wanted?" Robin shook his head. "An office?" she asked. "Room for all your gizmos and gadgets?" Robin shook his head again. "No, it's too important for that," he said. "It's going to be our bedroom."

Three days later the deal on the house was closed. Robin knew he could have haggled over the asking price. But didn't. A week later the first builders arrived. Followed by an architect. And a designer. And Gillian.

With sketches and floor plans and books and maga-zines and bundles of material, Gillian supervised each

34

detail. Back in her own country after five years – "in the wilderness, talk about forty days and nights" – she was ecstatic. She created The House. Years later in Goa it was "let's get those curtains for The House". Or on the island of Mykonos it was "those rugs would work in The House". She wanted to live nowhere else. Nor did he. And all who entered the building soon commented on its warmth and tranquillity and comfort. A pattern of bricks and mortar arranged a century earlier seemed destined to wait for her arrival. The House was better for Gillian being its chatelaine.

On the day they moved in, she was guiding Robin from room to room, pointing out the changes made and asking for his approval, already indicating what she had in mind for the next stage of renovation and accepting that which could not yet be altered. "We'll block off the minstrel gallery. For now it's a cupboard. For now."

Michael, still a toddler then with a dummy forever in his mouth, sat astride her hip as she lugged him from room to room. Robin would always be able to recall the vision of her that summer's day. A light cotton dress folded over her bosom, revealing just enough to keep him aware. Long black hair gathered at the back. That smiling, happy, healthy face supported by an elegant never-ending neck. Somewhat disproportionate really, that neck, too long, but it all added to her startling attractiveness. "Your best feature is your neck," he had told her often. Although he also loved the broad expanse

of skin gently fleshing out her shoulders, loved the feel
of them on those nights when he took her from behind.
Gillian started to shove aside the million props dumped
by the movers on Michael's bed. She laid Michael down
on his favourite blanket. And he was soon showing signs
of sleepiness. Gillian then drew the curtains on Samuel
who could be seen exploring the enormity of the jungle
that would one day be a back garden. And turned to
her husband.

Her: "Let's fuck in every room in the house."

Him: "That's a cliché."

Her: "So's fucking."

And so they did.

Robin drove home from the hospital slowly. Slowly
because clouded eyes could mean clouded judgement.
And because traffic dictated only an oozing pace. Motor-
ists' horns pushed him to advance at the allotted speed
through the asphalted inches of Hammersmith Broadway. He tried to ignore them. But a persistent hooter
in the adjacent lane demanded his attention. The driver
was young, no more than seventeen, and sounded his
horn off at a council rubbish truck that had stopped
without notice in front of him, then at Robin for being
next to the truck, and at each and every car that dared to
be on the same road at the same time as this young man.

Robin stared at him. The young driver was mouthing to no one in particular, not daring to catch the eye of other drivers, and with a hand continually rat-a-tatting on the horn. Hecuba, thought Robin, Hamlet.

> What would he do
> Had he the motive and the cue for passion
> That I have?

When he kissed Gillian goodbye she had clung to his jacket a trifle longer than usual. She wanted something. Through the years this arresting of his movements had always startled him, leading him to expect some awesome request, but what followed was usually mundane — a new book, to see a play in town, a dinner party.

"Can I decorate The House?" she asked. "Not the whole house," she added quickly, "just a few rooms. I know money's tight. But if I could . . ."

"Sure thing, kid," said Robin, "good idea. Needs doing."

She flung her arms around him. A tight clasping. He closed his eyes. He wanted to talk. In a hospital bedroom a husband and wife should be able to talk. About today. About tomorrow. Let's talk about tomorrow.

He could say nothing.

And Gillian said nothing.

She pulled out of his arms. He kissed her. "Goodnight, my wife."

"Goodnight, my husband."

"See you tomorrow."

"Yes, tomorrow."

Tomorrow. The thought of tomorrow can be terrifying. Not to Gillian. But it was to Robin.

When he reached the door, Gillian said, "Hey, mister, cheer up. It's only life."

"Oh, is that all it is?" said Robin. "I thought it was something serious."

"Nah," said Gillian, "finding new wallpaper, now that's serious."

An opening in the traffic. And the young horn blaster tried to cut in front of Robin. Realized he couldn't, was forced to brake. Robin made space for the young man's car. Then with a sweeping gesture signalled the youth to pull away in front of him. That made the young driver even angrier. The horn sounded non-stop.

Robin began to laugh. Still fighting tears.

CHAPTER

4

Michael watched his father wetting the green leaves of the sweetcorn before he spoke.

"Steve's father barbecues corn in foil," said Michael.

"Good for Steve's father," said Robin. "I don't. Is his corn better than mine?"

Michael shuffled. "Well, noooooo ..." he admitted reluctantly.

"Get me some more sauce from Mum, please." Michael was saved from this chore by Aunt Vanessa appearing with a large bowl of the brown liquid.

"Here it comes!" said Vanessa. Michael escaped to the other end of the garden.

Robin brushed the thick sauce onto the roast.

"What is the secret of Gillian's sauce?" asked Vanessa.

"Ketchup, Tabasco, Worcestershire, garlic — lots of garlic — lemon, paprika, Balsamic vinegar, fresh rosemary," said Robin, "it's none of those. It's my wine. Gillian is dyslexic when it comes to cooking wine. Never uses the plonk I get from Marks or Majestic, no, she manages to find the Margaux from the Wine Society. An '82 or '83 Margaux will improve any roast."

Robin turned the spit's motor off. Locked the joint into position. The sauce was sealing itself, darkening, into the meat. Occasionally the hot fire spat back drippings of fat with a flare of smoke and flame, but on the whole the barbecue was behaving itself.

"Looks good," said Vanessa.

"How was the skating?"

"The boys did well," said Vanessa, "considering they never see ice. Not like we folk on the Tyne. Or you, as a child."

"I can't remember what age I started," said Robin. "Dad tied a cushion to my tuss. Gave me a kitchen chair, one of those old metal chairs, for me to push around the ice. I held on, held on. He'd laugh a lot when I'd fall. Then one day I didn't fall."

They were interrupted by the raised voices of children. The correct position for dessert spoons was the subject. The garden table was being set for lunch. Samuel's friend, Matthew, who had arrived unannounced, was trying to arbitrate, unsuccessfully. All three glanced towards Robin. The shouting stopped.

"They're good boys," said Vanessa.

"I know," said Robin.

Gillian tapped her way out of the back corridor, a boat of salad dressing in one hand, a three-pronged walking stick in the other.

"Mum, I can do that," shouted Samuel, intercepting her.

"Thank you," said Gillian. "And the salad's ready, on the kitchen table."

"Mike, get the salad," Samuel ordered.

"His name is Michael," said Robin and Gillian almost together.

"I know, I know, sorry," said Samuel, then added, "Isn't it time you guys had a drink?"

The adults agreed. Vanessa asked for a dry sherry, Robin and Gillian for white wine.

"The French or the Australian?" said Samuel.

"Surprise me," said Robin.

"And, Dad, shall I cut up some kohlrabi?" asked Samuel.

"Perfick!" replied Robin, imitating the H.E. Bates character.

"He loves munching raw veg," Samuel explained to Vanessa, "especially when drinking." Then added, laughing, "A healthy alcoholic."

"Thank you!" Robin shouted after the boy disappearing into the house.

Gillian came close to the fire and Robin. "Nigel and Mary just rang. They can't make it," she said. Robin shrugged, poked the fire. "Better see about the caramelized carrots," said Gillian. "He likes cooked vegetables too."

She made her way back to the kitchen.

"Who are Nigel and Mary?" asked Vanessa.

"He's a commercials director, she's a PA. Supposed to come to lunch," said Robin. "We haven't seen them for months. More. Not since Gillian's been ill. She and Mary used to be close, well, close-ish. Now, a card at Christmas, the obligatory card. They don't write. Don't phone. She insisted on asking them. I'd see them in hell."

"Robin, you must understand, be forgiving," said Vanessa.

"Forgiving? No, that's for you lot. Turn-the-other-cheekers. Christians. Believers. Not for me. Not for atheists. I can go on hating as long as I want. Understanding? Well, I think I understand all right. Disease reminds us we're all vulnerable. We're all going to die. One look at Gillian and you see how frail we are. So avoid seeing her. But that's my wife ... A woman, their friend, is now a leper." He locked the roast into another position. "Others have been wonderful, y'know. Richard and Annie across the road. Peter and Millicent. Hugh and Rohan. Geoffrey, Alan. Stronger than ever.

"The friends thou hast and their adoption tried,
grapple them to thy soul with hoops of steel.

"The rest. Shits. All of them. I saw Maurice the

42

other day, in Piccadilly. You've met them, haven't you, Maurice and Pru? Smiling, he was. Came towards me, hand forward for shaking. Smiling. We were really close at one time. And when Pru's Mom died, Gillian was there for days. Other things, practical things. Poker games, the school run, kids and problems, mortgages and problems, fornicating and problems. Long talks into the night. Now all is silence." He added more sauce. "I didn't shake his hand. I was polite. Gillian's motto. 'You're a *gentle* man, so always be a gentleman.' Advice to a wild colonial boy from a civilized girl. Hah ... But I didn't shake his hand."

When Samuel returned with the drinks he brought a long extension into which he plugged an electric carving knife.

"That's clever," said Robin.

"Mum's sauce deserves the best," said his son.

"What about my cooking?"

"Needs all the help it can get," said Samuel.

Robin faked an imaginary swipe across Samuel's head. The boy ducked and called out to his brother. "C'mon, Mike – Michael – wash your hands. You too, Matthew."

Matthew, a thin-faced, red-haired boy, came closer to the barbecue to inspect the offerings. He looked down at the roast simmering succulently over the charcoals. His mouth twisted. "I thought we were going to McDonalds," he said.

43

CHAPTER

5

By the time they got to the restaurant it was late even for Paris. When Robin stopped at the hotel's front desk for a quick thumb-through of the *Guide Michelin* and other such books, Clara tested and retested the locks on her stowed bags. Eventually she determined them worthy to be let out of her sight. Robin hid a smile. After a brief chat with the concierge about the local offerings, he appeared to be satisfied. "Most important decision of the day," he told Clara, "where to dine." Clara let him lead her there.

The throb of Saturday night bounced off the pavements to envelop them. Clara's eyes darted about observing well-dressed women and casually dressed men, boys, girls, agreers, arguers, singles, families, children, babies, shouters, cuddlers, haters, lovers, groups of twos and threes and fours and fives coming at her in waves, and clusters of people blocking pavements and forcing her and Robin into the path of tooting cars. Saturday night. Live.

Robin saw the sparkle in her eyes. "Definitely not San Diego," he said.

"Definitely not," she replied. She threaded her way past garbage and past people, stepped over the water and pipes forever running along Paris gutters into sewers.

In the restaurant Robin asked for two *couverts*. The head waiter peered over half-glasses to look at Clara from toe to head in slow and frank appreciation.

"Are you sure it's for two?" he asked in English, looking only at Clara. "Perhaps mams'elle would consider an alternative? I have a superb table for one, for example ... No? Well, in that case follow me."

Mahogany surrounds contrasting with white linens, sparkling crystal, reflecting silverware, and Robin suspected, as they sat, this was a good place to have fallen into. The waiters were almost too attentive, opening Clara's napkin with a flourish and watching as she spread it nervously over her lap.

"You choose," she half-whispered as the large menus arrived.

Robin was about to protest but then decided not to. She'd been travelling more than half a day, eating food that had been microwaved into mush. "Something fresh?" he suggested. She nodded. "You okay on shellfish?" he asked. She nodded even more enthusiastically.

45

"Two *fruits de mer*," Robin told the waiter who went off happily. "You'll like it," he assured Clara. "Now to drink. Champagne? Claret?"

"It's fish so it has to be white," she stated flatly. Robin smiled. "That's what they say," she insisted.

"It doesn't have to be anything," said Robin. "Except something you'd like." Her creased brow showed she wasn't convinced. "Actually, I prefer red," he added.

"Can it be red?" she asked.

From an over-burdened list Robin chose a medium-weight claret. And assured her that gourmets and gourmands throughout this food-loving nation would forgive them. "But only if we really enjoy it," he said.

The three-tiered platter of shellfish embedded on snowy ice, magnificently arrayed, arrived at the table. Clara recognized the clams, the oysters, the mussels, but queried the langouste — "the lobster without claws" — the crab, the scallops, the snails, and the prawns that ranged from jumbo to shrimps. Like a good child trying to please a watching parent, she tried them all. And wondered why the oysters were saltier than the Pacific variety. Why some snails were so much tastier than others. And why she had never eaten raw mussels before. And laughed. And drank. And talked.

"How old are you?" asked Robin.

Clara paused before answering. "You're not supposed to ask."

46

"Another one of the rules?" he asked.

She sipped her wine. "I'm twenty-eight."

He was relieved. He'd thought she might be younger. "And not married?" he asked.

"I lived with a man for three years."

"And?"

"I left him about a year ago."

"Why?"

"I didn't want him to be the father of my children." She paused. "Took a while for me to know that, but when I did, I left."

"Tell me about him," said Robin. Clara shrugged but would say no more.

"Bet his name is George," added Robin.

"Why George?" she asked.

"Every Tom, Dick and Harry is called George," said Robin. "What's he like?"

She paused. "He said it has to be white wine with fish."

Robin nodded. "Oh," he said slowly, "*that* George!" Clara laughed.

Robin rarely ate dessert. But convinced her to have an *île flottante*.

"What is it?" she asked.

"I dunno. Gooey. Meringue, in a sort of syrup. You'll like it."

"How do you know?"

Because my children like it and you're older but

47

not that much older, thought Robin, but only said, "I just know."

When she tried it she liked it so much that Robin soon ordered another. And watched her revel in a blissful excess of sweetness. Meanwhile he munched on his salad which he enjoyed having, European style, after the main course.

"You must have children," she said.

"Two. Boys."

"How old?" she asked.

For a split-second Robin debated about lying, since to make the boys younger might make him appear younger. But decided to tell the truth.

"Samuel is sixteen. Michael fourteen . . . No, thirteen. Soon fourteen."

"Is your wife really sick?" she asked.

Robin nodded.

"Do you want to tell me about it?"

Robin paused, then said, "No."

Coffee arrived.

"Don't you want to know my age?" he asked.

She looked into his eyes for some time. "No," she said, simply.

Parades of people still marched up and down the boulevards and avenues. It was decided to join them for a short walk first, to the Place de l'Opera, then resume the hunt for a hotel. Clara strode, California style, not caring what separated her from Robin as the surrounding herds pushed and shoved between them, making many a young buck think she was alone, which led to gestures and comments until it was realized she was escorted. In the end, to save any possible problem Robin took her arm. Clara did not seem to mind.

At a sidewalk café, where Robin insisted on stopping, she ordered coffee while he asked for a malt. Behind them a chanteuse, phoneticallly forcing her tongue into foreign shapes, sang.

> It had to be you
> No ozher would do
> I vandered arownd
> And finally foun'

The waiter arrived with the drinks, shoved the little chit under a saucer, and hovered over them aggressively until Robin paid.

"I'd forgotten they do that," said Clara. "Can I pay for mine?"

"You can't pay for anything," Robin replied, "but don't stop offering." Clara smiled. That she was travelling on a budget and didn't resent expensive Paris being paid for by someone else was now apparent.

"What do you do in San Diego?" he asked.

"Machinery. For making glass."

"Sales?"

"No, maintenance."

Robin was puzzled. "You wear overalls, get covered in grease, wield a monkey-wrench, a screwdriver and ..."

"If a machine breaks down," Clara explained tolerantly, "I send an engineer out. All over. Including your London. It's a large department. We're big. I run it. You have to know a lot about the machinery. And I do."

She enlarged on the mechanics of glass making. This time not even her animated lip movements could make it sound interesting. He couldn't think about the machines. He thought about her lips.

"You're in personnel?" he asked. "Now called 'human resources'. Pompous phrase."

"It is, isn't it?"

"I thought you might be in the arts," he said.

"Because you are?" she asked. "Are you?"

"Sort of," he replied, "advertising."

"Almost the arts," she joked. "Doing what exactly?"

For a reply he walked to a nearby newspaper kiosk to buy a copy of the *Financial Times*. Found the ad. Folded over the page. And plopped it in front of her. Clara saw a series of Russian dolls, each revealing another doll hidden within itself in the usual fashion, until the final doll, more eye-catching and colourful than the rest, revealed a bottle of a new brand of vodka.

"My idea, my campaign," said Robin flatly, not

boasting. Any thought of bragging about his work had been exorcized long ago by Gillian.

"Hardly going to feed the hungry in Alabama, is it? Or move one kid out of a tin hut in Naples!"

He remembered her face, menacing, close, flecked with anger and alcohol, shouting at him.

"The only kids I have to worry about are the two sleeping upstairs," he'd said, breaking away from the confrontation to close the bedroom door. The argument had started, as it often did, as they were preparing for bed, half-naked bodies provoking half-naked words.

"If you're so worried about your kids why did you spend so much time with Margot whatever-the-hell-her-name is?" asked Gillian.

Then Robin, understanding, began to laugh. Gillian, at first reluctantly and then despite herself, also began laughing. And came towards him with a face now layered with night cream. And they hugged and kissed. Ignoring the cream.

"You could be lying." Clara brought him back to Paris. "You could be making the whole thing up."

"Not very trusting, are you?" said Robin, noting the smile in soft eyes. "Where did that happen? San Diego or Paris?"

"Tsk, tsk." Clara tutted at him. "There you go again. Using the word 'very'." She vamped him with her eyes. "I believe you," she said.

She sipped from her cold cup, refusing another, after

admitting she neither liked nor often drank coffee. Bit of a kvetch, thought Robin. Lovely. But a kvetch. Too goodie-goodie. He bit his lip. No, don't knock her. Don't denigrate, he told himself. Don't look for imperfections as you often do to justify not pursuing the quarry. For not continuing the chase. She's only human. And young. And female. Continue. He said nothing. And they sat and watched the crowds pass the café. Aware that the mood was changing. Saturday night energy was dissolving into Sunday morning lethargy.

Clara told him about her father, a German who managed to get out from behind The Wall and came to the States where he met and married her American mother, whose background was indeterminate, though probably Waspish. She described the marriage as "ordinary" and "just like any other". And was not put out when Robin said there was no such thing. She made no further comments on the marriage except to say it produced two other children, her brothers. "Ordinary. Just ordinary," she repeated.

"Do they love each other?" asked Robin.

"Does anybody?" she replied.

"Yes," he said simply.

Clara said nothing.

"At least people know about the downside," he said. "If they don't love each other, they know it. You found that out. That man you lived with. 'George'. Isn't that what happened with you and George?"

For something to do, while she thought about this, she brought the now empty coffee cup to her mouth.

"Do you love your wife?"

"Yes."

"Much?"

"Yes, much. A lot of 'muchs'. A lot," he said.

Clara again said nothing.

He finished his whisky. "Let's find you a hotel," he said.

CHAPTER

6

"I feel like that bottle of Liebfraumilch," said Gillian as she returned to sit beside Robin in the empty waiting room having been through, yet again, another series of hospital tests. It was a reference to younger days when every invitee felt it necessary to bring a bottle of wine to a party, a sort of unspoken price of admission. As the party dwindled to an end and the need for more wine sparked off a search amongst the empties, one unopened bottle, more often than not a sweet German wine, could still be found, its label betraying just how bad its contents would be. It would remain unopened. To be found by the party's hosts the next morning. And they would put it on a shelf, until another invitation to another party meant that it could be passed on to a new pair of unsuspecting hosts. Never opened, never drunk, simply passed on.

"You're much too dry to be a Liebfraumilch," said Robin.

"Thank you, darling." She squeezed his arm. Is she as frightened as I am? Robin wondered. It was so hard to tell with Gillian. But why had Professor Knights sent for them? "Chardonnay, am I? Or Chablis?" she asked.

"I think I ordered Liebfraumilch on our first date," said Robin.

"No," she protested, "we wouldn't. You wouldn't. Not even then!"

What horrors would the young professor spring on them this time? Last year on one of these after-hours visits, Knights, while Gillian was dressing in another room, took Robin aside and blurted out, "You must not expect your wife to see in the New Year." What a blow to the stomach that was, no, a knife in the stomach, no, a cleaver in the stomach, causing a deep scarring pain. That was in October. And now it was March. And Gillian was still here. Stooped. Crippled. Rounded. But still my woman, my wife, still sitting beside me. Talking about Liebfraumilch.

"Kids like sweet things," said Robin, "candy before caviar. Hock first, claret later."

The waiting room was like a summer resort out of season. Empty. Bereft of hordes. Robbed of tumult. Unaccustomed silences. Unpeopled spaces. And, as in a deserted resort, the emptiness was wrong, eerie and frightening.

A pair of nurse's heels clattered by breaking the silence. As did occasional distant sounds. Hollow voices. From hollow rooms. Doctors. Orderlies. Patients coughing. Always patients coughing. Doors closing. Or opening. Far away. Echoing softly into the waiting room.

Gillian unconsciously played with a bit of torn vinyl on the bench. "I think it was Verdicchio. Or Lacrima Christi. That's as close as I get to religion. Lacrima Christi, the tears of Christ, in a bottle."

Robin looked at her pinched face. Too thin, anorexically thin.

"Caught the stunner in the draughting room yet?" asked the voice from the past. Madison Avenue. Decades ago. "English. Nice," said the informant. And Robin could remember himself, the young executive, newest member of Kohler & King, in short-sleeved shirt, tie tucked in, a cigarette packet under a rolled-up sleeve adding to the bulge in his muscles, devising a reason for visiting the artists' department. And seeing her. Three weeks later, a date. Eleven months later, a conversation. "I'm not going to your house for Christmas unless I go as your fiancée." Ultimatum time. "I went to the Cape for that weekend. Your family's okay, but—" Gillian trying hard not to cry, and succeeding. "You're so sure," Robin remembered asking, "about us ... that you and I ...?" Gillian in his arms. Looking intently at him. "I am sure. Sure." And so to Christmas dinner. And to betrothal. And the rest.

Robin looked at his watch. The summoning by the professor, the call from Gillian, the gut-grabbing fear, the cancelling of the day's appointments, again — "Tell Peter I'll make it up to him", shouted to a secretary — in the car to collect her, finding a parking space near the hospital and then at last arriving at the ward. Made it. Only to be told, "Oh, you needn't have rushed, we'll be ages yet." Gillian goes off for tests. Returns. And now the waiting. The endless, boring, futile waiting. Waiting in a waiting room. Where else?

"Does anybody still drink that stuff?" asked Robin, after another glance at his watch, "Verdicchio and Lacrima Christi. Nowadays it's all Pinot Grigio, Frascati and—"

"Chianti," said Gillian. "Still see Chianti around. Though I haven't seen those wicker bottles for some time."

"Thank heavens," said Robin.

Gillian smiled. "Must've been an Italian wine. On our first date. Had to be . . . At least, let's say so." She took his hand. And Gillian and Robin waited.

"Officially you are in remission," said Professor Knights. "The disease appears to have halted."

His eyes blinked repeatedly. He appeared to speak the words reluctantly, almost sounding disappointed, certainly puzzled. "We're never completely sure why it happens. Just that it happens. Sometimes. If we're lucky," said the young professor. Robin looked over at Gillian. She was not elated. But looked intently across the desk at Knights.

"I drove my car yesterday," she said in almost a whisper. "I didn't want to tell you, darling," she turned to Robin. "No one saw me. No one. None of our neighbours. Not Annie across the road. Not our two guys. Not a postman. Or a dustman. Street was empty. No one 'keeping an eye on Gillian'. Felt like a truant, no, more like an escapee. Sneaking to my own car, unlocking the door, sitting, adjusting mirrors. Starting the engine. Wondering if I dare. Dared. Only round the block. But I drove my car."

A pause. Again all that could be heard were far-away hospital noises. And Robin's breathing.

"Yes," said Knights after a moment, "your energy is coming back."

"I knew it," said Gillian. "I knew it." She crunched the handkerchief in her hand.

"How long will this remission last?" asked Robin. Gillian winced. Damn, thought Robin, she'd rather not know the answer to that question. But she did not attempt to stop Knights from answering.

"No way of knowing," said Knights, "days, maybe weeks, months, years even, if we're lucky."

"Oh, we're lucky," said Gillian. And pushed herself

up from her seat. For her the meeting was over. "Always lucky. Aren't we, darling?" She linked her arm into Robin's.

"I still want to see you," said Knights, also rising. "Say every month or so. Of course you can call me. Whenever you like."

Gillian offered her hand. "I want to thank you. For everything."

As Robin watched, the professor of medicine took Gillian's hand and pressed it gallantly to his lips. Yes, thank him, thought Robin. Thank him for the radiotherapy that's crippled your bones. Thank him for the chemotherapy that's burned your hair and washed away God knows what juices your body needs. Was it all necessary? Was it the right thing to do? Maybe it was all mumbo jumbo. Witch doctors. In high-rise glass towers.

"I'm delighted," said Knights. "You've been so good. After that long course of radiotherapy. Then the chemotherapy. So good. I'm delighted." And then added, too tolerantly, "Of course, I know you subscribe to alternative medicine as well."

Gillian took her hand away. "Why is it called 'alternative'? If it helps me?" Robin flushed with admiration for her, standing up to the doctor, even now, refusing to be put into the submissive patient's role.

"Of course you're absolutely right," blustered Knights.

"Maybe," continued Gillian, "you should meet my Chinese doctor."

Robin guffawed.

"Sorry," he said, stifling his laughter. Gillian and the professor stared at him. But the thought of the white-coated professor who took himself so seriously meeting the flamboyant Asian whose apparel consisted of multi-coloured cloths on multi-checked garments was laughter inducing. Yes, set the tomtoms going. Let the two shamans meet. They had so little in common they must be made for each other. Professor Knights disdainfully wrote out prescriptions. These were handed on to the hospital's pharmacy who, sometimes up to an hour or more later, produced the pristine packets. Whereas the colourful Dr Sang disappeared into a back room and emerged with dusty bottles of pills, packets of teas of all kinds – usually torn – and bags of herbs, an endless number of herbs. Which Gillian would brew into a foul-smelling liquid – stinking up the house – that resulted in a tea or a soup that was even more foul to the tongue. Knights spoke in voluptuous vowels forced past nasal tones. Dr Sang spoke quickly and undecipherably, having to repeat himself many times in order to be understood. For some reason he had no one in his office to translate Mandarin to his bemused patients. Knights was taciturn. Dr Sang never stopped talking. Was the ebullient Dr Sang a talent or a charlatan? Robin was never sure. But, Robin learned, he had a conventional doctor's degree from the University of London even though he preferred to practise Chinese medicine. And he too had earlier taken Robin aside and said, or attempted to say, "What your wife has, she has. I cannot fix what has hurt her. But I can stop the cancer. She will get no worse." Robin had stood eyeball to eyeball appraising him. Rogue or saviour, which are you, Dr Sang? Most important was Gillian's opinion. "He makes me feel good," said Gillian. And that was reason enough for the two of them, arm in arm, together, always together, to chance the perilous steps down to an office in Shepherds Bush — hah, what a name! Robin still revelled in the uniqueness of English names — to see the hyperactive Chinese doctor.

"Yes," said Knights, "perhaps you'd ask Doctor ... Sang ... is that his name? ... to call me." The brush-off. Polite. Patronizing. But certainly a brush-off. Knights had never been interested in analysing the medicines the Chinese physician prescribed.

"Get the morphine down to sixty mil," said Knights, then added, "if you can."

To fight the pain Gillian took morphine twice a day. She was allowed to vary the amount according to her needs, a sign of trust between her and Knights, although she always reported the dosage to the hospital. At each visit to see the professor a new prescription was collected for more morphine tablets. Beige tablets were 10 milligrams in strength. Pink, 30. Blue, 60. And grey, 100. Like a colourful collection of candies. Sweets for the suffering.

Gillian took eighty milligrams of morphine for each dose. When she and Robin tried to reduce the amount, the pain would return. And that was not allowed. "Never let the pain break through!" Knights had once admonished Gillian for tolerating some unbearable aching she need not have suffered. "Pain weakens the patient," said Dr Lundt, the family doctor, "making it harder for you to fight!"

"We tried. Tried getting it down from eighty," Robin explained to Professor Knights. "We can't. As it is she can hardly wait for the evening dosage."

Knights merely nodded. "You have enough of everything else?" he asked.

Morphine cannot be taken on its own. Other drugs must be taken to counteract the morphine's harm. A drug to settle the stomach. A drug to fight the nausea. A drug to stop the constipation. And more. It was this supply of secondary medicines that Professor Knights was checking.

"Yes," said Robin, "we have enough. For the moment." Two shelves in Gillian's study were now devoted to heavy medicines. White boxes of morphine, MST, stacked alongside Zantac, Motillium, Lactulose, Aspav, Diconal, Diodenal and others. Each box carefully labelled, both by the chemist's precise typing and, in her large scrawling writing, by Gillian so that the strength and usage – "when vomiting take two" – reduced the exotic names into more familiar terms.

"I wish you well," said Knights. The professor of medicine stood, a silhouette framed in the doorway, watching them depart.

"Tea shop closes at four o'clock," came from the large black face of an attendant hovering threateningly over Robin. It was a few minutes past four.

"We don't want anything, just sitting," said Robin placatingly.

"Hmmph," the attendant hmmphed. And left.

Robin and Gillian sat, in the canteen balcony cantilevered over the main floor of the hospital, and watched as the activities below them began to increase now that the afternoon was stretching towards evening.

"Tonight?" asked Robin, "River Café, Stephen Bull's, or out to the country, to Raymond Blanc's? Or——?"

"Give me a kiss," said Gillian. He leaned across the hard, functional tabletop. And kissed her. Half on the cheek and half on the mouth. Then sat back. Gillian breathed deeply before she spoke.

"I want," said Gillian simply, "to go to Marks & Spencer." Robin smiled. "Without you." Robin looked worried. "Without Annie. Without a keeper. Without anyone. Alone . . . I'm going to make chicken cacciatori, Michael's favourite, and get that silly ice cream for Samuel, and you're going to open a bottle of that '82

Médoc, even if I can only have a sip, and . . . I want to
go shopping, to buy food . . . chicken and spaghetti and
onions and purée and . . . I'm going shopping. Alone.
Alone . . . Alone." Her voice drifted softly away.

He kissed her again. This time properly. Holding her
in his arms, ignoring others passing by or bustling below
him. Ignoring shopkeepers setting out stalls for the
evening trade. Ignoring outsiders, shaking cold rain from
coats on entering the hospital, anxious to be allowed
into the wards early, before the scheduled visiting
hour. Flush-faced delivery men with flowers and fruit
and baskets and boxes rushed towards closing elevator
doors. A young houseman and a nurse, white uniforms
under dark tweed coats, talking loudly and laughing
loudly, returning after some afternoon assignation — a
late lunch, or an early dinner, or half hour in a bedroom,
or a movie — stopped near them and the doctor almost
pointed a finger, almost spoke, to interrupt what to him
was the sight of two geriatric heads snuggled together,
when the nurse gently but determinedly led him away.
Robin kissed Gillian. And held her in his arms.

Robin could see Gillian as usual waiting under the
canopied glass doors of the hospital entrance. She
spurned the opened passenger door.

"Move over," she said.

Robin chortled. "May I see your driving licence, madam?" he asked, sliding along the seat.

"No, officer, you may not," said Gillian, adjusting her belt. "It has my age, my real age, in it. And only my husband knows that."

The car pulled away. Out of the hospital gates. Gillian turned to him and said, "Soon I'll be driving you to the airport again."

CHAPTER

7

"Je regrette, m'sieur," said the plump concierge, smugly folding arms under large breasts, not hiding her contempt for foreigners who didn't know the rules and tried to book a room so late at night. Five hotels all gave the same answer. Paris on the last Saturday night before the August exodus did not have space for this child from California. No room at the inn. Robin looked at Clara. Hardly biblical, though the white of her costume would contrast well with brown stable walls. Must make sure when we shoot the scene, he thought, to backlight her golden hair. Blonde in the manger.

Getting drunk, he told himself. Don't. But if she can't find a room. She'd have to stay with me. Oh God, please. Please.

"Can we get a taxi?" asked Clara. Outside, on the pavement in front of this last hotel, she stood biting her lip, scanning the abandoned streets. Not a taxi was in sight. "*Paris en août,*" she said. "How do you say 'empty'? Oh yeah. *Vide. Pas de taxi.*"

"Let's go back to my hotel," suggested Robin, "and phone from there."

They walked in silence for a few beats. When Robin tried to take her hand she eased away.

"I'm not going to spend the night with you," said Clara.

"Of course not," replied Robin.

A small smile as she asked, "No argument?"

"Would it do any good?" Robin asked.

"No," she said.

"Well then . . ." He shrugged.

More walking. In silence. No more words. Listening to heels clacking against cobblestones, water gushing along gutters, voices from nearby streets, and the ever-present sound of scooters.

Robin stopped. And looked down at her. "I want to say something," he said. He put a hand on each of her arms and pulled her towards him. She resisted stiffly and awkwardly. When her body was close to his, she looked up at him, apprehensively. "I want," he continued, "to say thank you for having dinner with me." She relaxed. He put his arms around her and kissed her. A long kiss. It was Robin who broke away first and added two more delicate kisses under her left ear.

They walked again. This time Clara let him take her hand.

Back at the Hôtel Mercure, the teenager who had signed them in was no longer behind the desk, replaced by a thick-lensed dumpy little man who sweated enormous globs while rushing about doing his duties. This new concierge, with Robin standing across the desk urging him on and tipping him frequently, had phoned taxi station after taxi station, and company after company, with little success. Some promised to phone back. Some did. Saying they would try. Even the long drive to the environs of Orly airport, it seemed, was not enough to lure recalcitrant Parisian taxi drivers out on the streets at one o'clock this morning.

While all this phoning was going on, interspersed with the concierge's other duties such as delivering bottled water to various rooms, dealing with complaints about the heat – windows stuck – and handing out keys to various late returning customers, Clara paced in the empty bar-room next door. Back and forth alongside her luggage, which, Robin noted, she had carefully checked yet again upon their return to make sure no lock had been molested, Clara strode nervously, almost neurotically. Robin, leaning back against the desk, drank another whisky the willing but sweating concierge had brought him. And watched Clara. Up and down she paced, the tassels on her costume swaying like a trapped lion's mane. But it's only the male lion that has a mane. Stop drinking, he told himself.

"*Le matin* ..." Not used to dealing with foreigners, especially anglophone foreigners, the concierge spoke hurriedly, as if to get over the experience as soon as possible. "In the morning, plenty of taxis, but now ... I regret."

Robin looked at Clara who had stopped pacing to hear the concierge's news. The phone behind the desk rang. The little man, with drops of sweat marking his route, ran to answer. It was a taxi company, to report no success. "Should I keep on?" asked the concierge. Robin nodded. The concierge resumed dialling. Clara resumed pacing.

"We could try again outside," suggested Robin to her. "The main streets. Not too far from here. Rue Montmartre or Boulevard Haussmann or walk to ..."

Clara approached. And looked at him steadily. "Can I trust you?" she asked.

The softness of a feminine face enveloping weary eyes made Robin yearn to stroke her cheek with the back of his hand. He returned her gaze. "No," he replied firmly. A tinge of fear appeared on her face. Seeing it, Robin added, "You know by now whether you can trust me or not."

Then Clara said the words Robin had been waiting all night to hear.

"I'm tired," she said. "I need to lie down."

Robin put down his drink, tried to conceal his excitement – not too quick, move slow – helped her manipulate the overloaded baggage trolley into the elevator. Which lifted them towards his bedroom.

CHAPTER

8

"Can I have my house back?" Robin was shouting at the top of his voice. Gillian watched, amused. "Can I *please* have my house back?"

Workmen, already packing up to leave for the day having worked well into the evening, stared at Robin. Why was he shouting? Paint pots, glue pots, ladders, steps, trestles and planks, carpets old uncovered, carpets new wrapped in plastic, brushes, bags of nails, boxes of screws, sheets and rags of many stains, were among the things that littered his bedroom. But that was normal. Why shout? Obviously the master of the house had been drinking and was taking it out, unfairly they believed, on them.

Gillian led the unsteady Robin down to the study converted temporarily to a bedroom. The workmen, six in all, said "Goodnight, Mrs Laurent" in various tones and accents as they passed on the stairs, glad to escape from this madman to the more comprehensible bedlam of a pub. When Gillian had said she'd changed her mind and now wanted extensive work done on the main bathroom, the original builder had suggested specialists – in plumbing as in medicine – would have to be brought in, hence the number of workers.

Earlier that morning Robin's partner, Peter, had had a heart attack. Robin was in a meeting with a corporate client – fizzy drink, POWER, health-giving and "does you a power of good", whose sales were dropping – when the doors of the conference room were thrown open by a hysterical male junior calling Robin's name. Gillian, was of course Robin's first thought. When he learned it was Peter he was surprised and shocked. Peter was a fitness fanatic, a jogger, a squash player, with at least two BUPA medical check-ups per year. As he ran towards Peter's office, Robin was also aware of how relieved he was that this time it was not Gillian.

Peter lay slumped on his side half under the desk. Four or five staff fussed around him. Robin sent all but Peter's secretary away, learned that an ambulance had been called and, desperately trying to remember his Eagle Scout days in New Jersey, rolled a semi-conscious and lightly moaning Peter onto his back. He pushed his hand past the small amount of puke in Peter's mouth to make sure his breathing was unblocked. Loosened Peter's collar, tie, belt and took his shoes off. He then removed his own jacket and put it under Peter's head. All the time talking gently to him. "It's okay, Peter," said Robin, "you'll be okay, Peter."

"Just one thing more, don't ever — as you Yanks like to do — call me Pete or even worse Petey," Peter had said to him fifteen years ago, "or it's the end, finis, of our partnership." It was in Berkeley Square where Peter Andersen who worked for a large agency met with Robin Laurent who also worked, in New York, for a large agency. A deal was being formalized after this fourth meeting to create a small agency in the unsure and uncertain hope of one day being another large agency. Fifteen years ago. "Sure thing," Robin had replied, "Peter-baby."

The colouring of the tiles at Guy's Hospital was different from Charing Cross but the smells were the same. As were the not-quite-clean white smocks of doctors and nurses. Certainly the personnel wearing the smocks were interchangeable. Some haggard looks. Vacant stares. Very few smiles.

"Are you a relative?" asked an older doctor.

Millicent, Peter's wife, was in the room with her

husband, while the doctor and Robin talked in the corridor.

"No," said Robin. "Partner. And friend. Close friend."

"The prognosis is not good," said the doctor. "We've given him the drugs, all we can, but the heart could rupture, explode, at any moment. And then ..." Grey hairs fell across the doctor's brow as he gestured. "He'll never be the same, you know. If that heart were a building it would be condemned. He'll need a bypass at least. Not now, of course. Soon. The next few hours are crucial. If he survives that ..." The grey hairs shook again.

Peter lay in the hospital bed, an insect with antennae of wires and tubes pulsating to and from his body, the mask on his face a hard-shelled mandible for digesting oxygen.

Millicent protested but Robin insisted she needed a break. He was told of a pub nearby and assured they would be sent for if Peter's condition changed. The pub was surprisingly close. Bless the Brits, thought Robin, pubs and churches there when you need them. Since they were both struggling to survive maybe they should amalgamate. Tankards clinking liberally amongst the congregation would certainly help the digestion of many a parson's sermon.

For Millicent he ordered what he knew to be her favourite after-dinner drink, brandy and port. "But I haven't eaten anything," she almost giggled. "Drink it," he said. She did. He sipped a malt. Bit early to start drinking, but who knows how this day will end.

"I want to be there when he wakes," said Millicent, "*if* he wakes." She had not asked what the doctor had said to Robin. She seemed to know instinctively.

Robin nodded. Decided to make light of it. "Yes," he said, "he'll hate what he's wearing." Peter cared about his clothes to a ridiculous degree. He could spend hours deciding what to wear for a particular conference and then, while Robin waited, change his outfit completely for the meetings that followed. "That slime-green hospital gown does little for his complexion," continued Robin. "And as for fitting ..."

"Yes," interrupted Millicent, "Peter is fussy about his clothes. Fussy about everything. Except where he shoves his cock."

Such words coming from her Cambridge-educated mouth seemed strange to Robin, who had never heard Millicent speak that way before.

Millicent was vaguely titled and so well mannered that she never pressed the point. Her family had money. Position. And land. Somewhere in Somerset. Whereas her husband's grandfather had been a coal miner. Peter's father ran, never owned, a corner grocery shop in Bradford. When Peter got to Oxford, on a scholarship, he dropped his accent, learned the importance of appearance, and contrary to the trend at the time did not brag about his working-class background but let people assume otherwise. And people did. Robin and Gillian, and perhaps one or two others, knew the truth.

Millicent finished her drink. Stood up. And took Robin's hand. "You've been a good friend to him. To me. Thank you."

"I don't know about that," said Robin. "His workload. Maybe if I—"

"No!" she said sharply. Millicent was a tall woman, never a beauty, and as she got older and her face thinner, the epithet hatchet-face became more and more applicable. A hatchet with orifices. "You always worked harder than Peter. Twice as hard. I hated that. I wanted to speak to you about it. Almost did. Once. But was afraid Peter would find out. Maybe if he'd worked harder he wouldn't have had time to chase—" She couldn't finish. Like a high-rise building dynamited on television news, her tall structure disintegrated from the ankles upwards. Robin held the sobbing wife in his arms, comforting her as best he could. Other drinkers gave them a passing glance, then looked quickly away, embarrassed. After a while she pulled away from Robin, straightened her shoulders, and headed for the glazed doors.

Where she stopped. Kept her back to Robin. And said, "If he dies . . . when he dies . . . I don't know what I'll do. I don't . . ."

And left the pub.

*   *   *

Back at the office Robin tried to pick up the pieces
of the shattered day. In the boardroom the staff, all
twenty-two of them, from the highest to the lowest, some
sincerely concerned, others just glad for this variation
in the daily routine, gathered. Robin was told that
work in progress had continued throughout the day.
Cancelled appointments had been rescheduled. Robin
nodded and muttered his thanks. He then reported
on Peter, understating his partner's condition, saying
simply that Peter – "as you would expect" – would
not be returning for some time. Two younger account
executives were elevated to take over Peter's work. Backs
straightening visibly, this new senior twosome tried not
to smile too often but expressed oversolicitous concern
about Peter's health. And overpraised his abilities. Robin
ignored this. He said he wanted a detailed account of
every promotion and production on the company books.
"We'll do it now, openly. Not the best way to deal
with the creative process, I know, and I will see you
all privately later, but without Mr Andersen I have to
know what's going down with each of you. I'm sure you
understand."

Sandwiches and drinks appeared. The large boardroom table was soon covered. Charts and notes and
graphics fought for space with neatly plated food and

drinks of all kinds. Robin stayed with malt whisky. And drank too much of it.

At the house he could see Gillian watching from an upstairs window as he struggled out of the taxi. She was smiling. She always seemed to take some sort of perverse pleasure out of his being drunk, probably because it proved he was comfortable enough in their relationship to return to primitive man. Also, Robin was a fun-drunk, rarely aggressive, just wobbly.

"Supposed to have finished two weeks ago," said Robin, referring to the builders' men he had just shouted at. "Gonna be here for months yet, aren't they? Why don't they move in so I can charge 'em rent?" Gillian was undressing him, putting him to bed. One trouser leg was proving difficult.

"Come along, my spouse, soused," she said. It was a phrase she had used before. Just as this was a routine that had happened before. She twisted the trousers free.

When she got down to slowly slipping off his underpants, Robin, despite his haze, remembered other undressings after other drunken bouts. In the old days when she got to this stage she would put her mouth around his penis, and either bring him to climax, or use it as a prelude to other activities. Sometimes, as he lay on the bed naked, she would approach with therapeutic oils to rub his back from toe to head, then he would roll over, and gentle fingers would caress his front, finishing on his centre to masturbate him and she would watch fascinated as the sperm spewed over her hands.

But that was before the disease. If Gillian was remembering those former days as well, she showed no sign of it. She silently, though giggling, helped him into pyjamas.

"G'night, my spouse, soused," she said, turning out the light. She stopped in the doorway.

"Robin," she said.

He murmured.

"I love you," she said. And closed the door.

CHAPTER

9

"That's an awful lot of money," said Clara. A heap of French notes spread before Robin on the dressing table as he emptied his pockets. What do I tell her? he wondered. He had taken a mass of cash with him because he had intended, after dining at the Brasserie Flo, to buy a hooker that night.

It was more than two years since he and Gillian had made love. More than two years since he had made love. Period. Full stop. He never thought he would make such a statement, convinced his hormonal drive would propel him between the legs of some woman in some situation every few days of his life or at the very least every few weeks. He was still young. His body needs and wants had not dimmed. But when Gillian became ill, abstinence evolved as if a normal consequence. Although he knew he masturbated too much.

Los Angeles, Paris and Milan have the best-looking whores in the world. At least that was the opinion of clients and crews reporting to Robin. Robin was hardly one to research the matter but saw no reason to doubt it. His experience with prostitutes was measurable. And strictly in the past. Not because he was a prude or that worried about disease but because payment debased the act of love into an act of sex. And he avoided it.

But now his body told him he had no choice. His need for a woman was overwhelming.

"Can I be first?" her head nodded towards the bathroom.

"My mummy said ladies should always be first. In everything," said Robin.

Except for the fact that her luggage seemed to crowd them out of spare space, making movement in the small bedroom a considered achievement, they soon settled into a routine. Was it always so with male-female relationships? Like an old married couple, as if they had known each other for years, Clara and Robin prepared for bed. He allotted certain drawers to her and a dresser top. She opened three of her many bags to unpack. She appeared, though tired, to feel comfortable, safe behind the ordinariness of readying herself for the night. An occasional apprehensive glance towards Robin, nothing more. She went into the bathroom. Came out. Went in again. Came out again. Forgetting something, picking that something up, returning to her ablutions. Finally the bathroom door closed. And stayed closed for several minutes.

Robin cleared a chair and pulled it onto the narrow ledge that stood in for a balcony. He waited.

When she emerged Clara was not covered in facial cream as Robin half-expected but, with eye shadow, lipstick and all other make-up removed, looked shining clean. Her strong, well-featured face glowed with youth. And health.

She was wearing what appeared to be a polka-dotted tennis costume; short pants, short-sleeved jacket buttoned tightly in front all the way to her neck. That will be difficult to undo, thought Robin, but all he said was: "You look nice." She smiled, tolerant but weary.

In the bathroom Robin changed quickly into black pyjamas. Checked himself for offensive body odours. Could find none. He nevertheless washed under his arms, brushed his teeth, splashed some aftershave on his face then as an afterthought dabbed some on his pyjamas' front.

Clara was lying on her side in the narrow bed.

"You're supposed to say that I look nice too," said Robin.

Clara opened her eyes, nodded. Said nothing. She closed her eyes again.

Robin lay down beside her. Her back was to him. She was not covered. It was too hot for covering of any kind. The open windows allowed no coolness into

82

the room, only gusts of abrasive noise from motorbikes, motorscooters, motorcars, and shouts from their owners. Sleep was unlikely to be found in this bedroom.

Robin parted her hair. Clara appeared to stop breathing. The back of his hand caressed the back of her neck then moved down her body slowly, knuckles pausing only to accentuate her left shoulder blade, her waist, and stopping just as her bottom's cheek became her leg, then up the other side, this time palm first until he found her neck again. Clara stiffened a little. But since she said nothing he took it to mean at the very least uncertainty, but possibly compliance. Robin pulled her towards him. His lips pushed through hair to touch her neck from one side of her spine to the other, then under each ear, and onto her lobes. He then tongued into the aural opening. Clara stretched, pulling away slightly. Robin used the movement to turn her onto her back.

She lay before him. Vulnerable. Accessible. His.

He kissed her ear again. And his hand moved to undo the button near her breasts. Her hand closed on his to stop him. He brought his lips onto the breast nearest him and through the clothing of her pyjamas blew hot breath onto her nipple. He made the wet cloth wetter as his tongue rotated round and round. Then he sucked on the wet cloth, the nipple beneath it, until his teeth gently but continuously rubbed on the erect nipple.

Still she said nothing. He undid the button and moved onto the other breast where he twined fingers delicately round this resting nipple until it too rose. He pulled the pyjamas opening to one side for a clear view of the delicious mound and its rosy centre.

Beautiful. So beautiful. Young, firm, shapely, appealing, the breast seemed to stare back at him. How could such beauty ever become cancerous? Must be the work of a devil to make this part of the human body so vulnerable to disease. A means of torturing women. And men.

He took almost all of her breast into his mouth, releasing it slowly until tongue and teeth trapped the wet nipple. Then he gazed longingly at this wet tit.

Robin's hand moved down her front to find her pubis, where he gently teased the top of the hair, pulling on it, twisting it round his fingers. Until he heard her cry.

Was he too rough? Had the pulled hair hurt, rather than enticed? No, it wasn't that. Could it be the cry of desire? The whimpering of women, a sound he had heard so often before, usually accompanied by protestations to which any man would be a fool if he listened. No, it wasn't passion. It was fear. A cry of fear.

Robin stopped. Pushed himself to sit at arm's length away from her. Clara's soundless crying continued.

Robin left the bed, grabbed the whisky bottle, and headed back to the balcony. After a large swallow, he resolved, no matter how much she cried, to return to the bed. In a few minutes.

CHAPTER

10

"If you think I'm walking around with only one tit on my chest for the rest of my life, think again!" Gillian was standing, glaring at Mr Whitton, the surgeon.

Mr Whitton was the man who had removed her breast. Robin could never get over that fact. What sort of man is it who can take a razor and slice off a woman's breast? Not my sort of man, thought Robin. But what sort of God is it that diseases the loveable tissues of a woman's anatomy? The sort of God that makes men like Mr Whitton.

Harley Street. Muffled traffic noise was all that was allowed through the thickened windows of Mr Whitton's dark office. The surgeon was of the old school. A blue pinstripe suit, possibly from Savile Row, but more likely from Harrods; not quite a wing-collared shirt, almost, but not quite; and of course, a school tie.

When Gillian stood up in her anger to confront him, Mr Whitton of course rose as well. Robin remained seated.

Gillian leaned on the desk, raised her voice again. "I want a reconstruction," she said.

"I don't approve," replied Mr Whitton, trying to find a firm voice.

Gillian's eyes widened. "It's my body," she roared, "and I'll do with it what I want!" Mr Whitton knew better than to answer.

Two years before this scene had taken place, Gillian had presented herself to Mr Whitton with a lump in her left breast. He explained the operation that was to follow. While she was under the anaesthetic an incision would be made in the lump and then it would be analysed. If this biopsy confirmed the lump to be cancerous, a mastectomy, the removal of the breast, would take place.

"If it is cancer, how long would you expect me to live?" Gillian had asked.

"Hopefully five, or maybe six, years," Mr Whitton said.

"That's not enough!" Gillian shouted. "My boys, my sons, are babies. I need ten years!"

Taken aback, Mr Whitton said, "Well, we can't guarantee—"

"Ten years!" Gillian insisted.

Despite himself, the stuffy surgeon seemed to smile,

"Well then, I'm sure you shall have your ten years."

Gillian wanted the last word. "At least ten years," she said.

After the operation Gillian avoided revealing her chest to Robin. It was not a pretty sight. The symmetry of the human form demands twosomes in so much of its construction. Certainly in the shapeliness of female breasts, two was beauty, one was ugly, unseemly, a joke even.

> "Ain't it a pity,
> she's only one titty,
> to feed the baby on."

The schoolboy song. And what was once convex was now concave, rounded and outgoing had become collapsed and hollow. An ugly scar, starting from under the arm, zigzagged across her chest like a zipper on a flattened case now empty of the treasure it once possessed. The nipple, the rosy allure, gone. Occasionally a nightdress would slip or Robin came across her unexpectedly in the bathroom and both he and Gillian would carry on as if neither noticed. When they made love he would fondle her good breast, Sometimes, to show he was suffering with her, he tried to move towards the scar, but she took his hand away. At first the lovemaking after the operation was restrained but Gillian's passion soon took over and they made love as fulsomely as ever. With one difference. She kept her upper body covered.

Prosthetics for breasts, usually silk flesh-pink coloured shapes, are offered to women in various speciality shops. Or else sponges, firmer, more rounded, can be stuffed into the empty bra. "Is Modom a 34C or a 36a?" A stop in Knightsbridge, near Harrods of course — "where else would you buy a good tit?" — on the way back from the hospital after the mastectomy, where Gillian insisted on immediately buying a prosthetic. She thrust one into Robin's hand. "You won't get off sucking on these, will y', kid?" she whispered. The wisecrack to hide humiliation.

Gillian was a stunning dresser. And that did not change with the removal of one breast. Many an old dress, many an old top, was delivered to the local Oxfam shop. Gillian soon learned how to conceal her loss. So much so that at parties where she often dared to wear low-cut gowns, women, but mainly men — and even Peter — could be caught staring. Knowing she had a breast removed, they tried to discern where Gillian's natural cleavage left off and the false began. "Y'know, Frank," she raised her voice once to one of the most boring of balding neighbours, "you used to look me in the eyes!" Silence. Robin was the first to lead the laughter that followed. You don't mess with my wife, he thought, just 'cause she's got one boob.

But the prosthetics chafed her skin. Or would slip. With comic results. A sudden dash to the pub toilet on one of their too infrequent nights out. "I was going

Chinese," she explained on returning to the table. Robin looked puzzled. "Wun Hung Lo," said Gillian.

So it was inevitable that Gillian would demand the reconstruction of her body after less than two years. The problem was that Mr Whitton had not allowed for a flap of skin, as later became common in mastectomies, so that the breast could more readily be replaced.

The Harley Street trot. Not for the first time parading up and down Harley Street and Devonshire Street and Wimpole Street and all the other streets where posh plastic surgeons held offices, Gillian and Robin went searching for someone to restore her body to what it once was.

"Yes, I can give you a mound," said one Harley Street man patronizingly.

"A mound!" Gillian said, rising to leave. "Isn't that something for baseball players!" She pulled on her coat. "Or a garden? Or a graveyard? A mound!"

The surgeon watched her depart. "Your wife is very excitable," he said to Robin.

"Have you ever had a breast removed?" Robin asked. "And then replaced?"

The doctor bit his lip.

"Good day to you, sir," said Robin.

"I shall be sending you my bill in any case," said the surgeon, his voice louder.

"No doubt," said Robin. And left.

Back at the house, the new au pair girl with a broad

Dutch smile and a broad Dutch body, was putting the two children to bed. Gillian was cooking. Gillian insisted that she and Robin dined alone, promising the two boys, then aged four and six, that when they were older, in a year or two, they would always have dinner together. Robin's goodnight ritual to his two sons was fairly consistent. At Michael's door he let the Snoopy dog toy precede him into the room, making Michael guess exactly where on the door, side or top, Snoopy would next appear. All this accompanied by much barking and an imaginative imitation of how Snoopy would sound if a dog could talk. With Samuel he would sneak his hand onto the light switch, jiggle it up and down, mimicking thunder and lightning.

"What's the new girl's name?" Robin asked as he opened the wine.

"Magda," said Gillian, "don't tell me you fancy her."

"I fancy every woman."

"Especially," said Gillian, "if she lost about three stones."

"How much?" asked Robin. He calculated rapidly. "About forty pounds. That's about right." The wine cork popped out.

Robin often said Gillian was not a good cook; she was a great cook. That night she made osso bucco. Later her cooking was to become simpler with less meats and reduced sauces. But that was later on. Tonight the meal of veal on the bone was full-blooded with braised fennel and peperonata and gravolata – a garlicky green sauce Robin adored – and salad, followed by pears in vanilla. She cooked a proper meal almost every day. She liked cooking. She liked eating. Better still she liked the fact that Robin relished his food. "A man who no like-a ta eat, he no like-a ta fuck," she would say in mock Italian. Robin seemed to satisfy her on both counts.

Robin waited until the bottle of Vosne-Romanée was almost gone before he broached the subject. When he thought the delicious food and heady wine had mingled sufficiently to placate their spirits, he asked, "Darling, would you consider going to Switzerland or France for this operation? Or New York or Los Angeles?"

"Hollywood or bust," said Gillian, "wasn't that a slogan in the thirties? I'm sure you could use it. Suggest it at the office: 'Get your bust in Hollywood or bust'. Could be catchy."

After more talk, less frivolous, Gillian mentioned two or three supposedly world-famous actresses that Robin had never heard of – the current crop of film leading ladies he found unmemorable – who had undergone plastic surgery with disastrous results because it was so evident. Pacific Coast surgery, Gillian maintained, was not all that it was supposed to be.

So the Harley Street trot began once again. Trudging the streets of WI continued until they found Mr Laker. This surgeon would have been ideal cast as a senior member of an insurance firm. Round nose, round cheeks, big round eyes on a happy round face. He wore light grey suits and white shirts with broad grey stripes. His office was as light and cheerful as his banter.

He explained meticulously to Gillian what the operation to reconstruct her battered body would involve. A silicone implant to be covered by skin removed from her lower back. The nipple to be formed by roughing skin, taken from the same area, on top of which would be put a final coat to come from the existing nipple. "Fortunately you have a big nipple," approved Mr Laker.

"All his work," said Gillian, nodding towards Robin, "and his two sons kept up the family standard when I was breast-feeding them."

Scarring would be kept to a minimum near the buttocks. The front would be virtually flawless.

Gillian could hardly control her elation. "Sounds better than the Jag!" she said. Robin's car was an old Jaguar, envy of many friends and neighbours, even though it was constantly and expensively in the local garage being restored. As they left the medical man's office, Gillian was radiant. She hugged Robin, hugged Mr Laker and seemed to have to restrain herself from hugging the somewhat startled grey-haired nurse receptionist. Glowing with anticipation she floated back to the car. Her knuckles tapped the top of the Jaguar before entering. "Soon I'm goin' to be like you," she said, "an old crock, but worth keeping."

She spent more than seven hours on the operating table.

Immediately afterwards in her room, she opened heavy-lidded eyes to survey her bandaged body. She forced herself to speak.

"Am I me again?" she asked.

"You am," Robin replied.

Samuel and Michael were with Robin. The two boys stood respectfully still, stiff, upright, as if any movement might cause their mother needless pain. Both wore school uniforms. Adult jackets, short trousers, while the regulation beanie caps dangled beneath twitching fingers. The severity of the black flannel school costumes contrasted so completely with the gentleness of their childhood. To Robin they appeared to be a squad of two small soldiers standing at attention. Waiting for the moment to break ranks. But until then, formal. Disciplined. Though crying.

Gillian winked at them. "I bet I look like an Egyptian mummy," she managed to say slowly, referring to her bandages, "but I'm not. I'm just your mummy."

The stiffness broke. The boys ran to the bed. "Can we kiss her?" Samuel turned to ask his father.

"You'd better," Gillian replied for Robin, "I haven't gone through this, not to be kissed by handsome guys."

93

Carefully avoiding touching her body, Samuel leaned over the bed and kissed her. Robin held Michael aloft so that the child's lips could caress his mother. Gillian was asleep again by the time the kissing stopped.

Two years earlier, Robin had left his sons at home on that occasion, gone to the London Clinic on his own, and waited in the reception area for Mr Whitton to come down to tell him the result of the biopsy. And its consequences. It was strange to the point of weirdness to be waiting near the hospital doors while such ordinary things happened as the world entering and exiting wearing the flowing robes of Arabia or the striped suits of The City or the bright shirts of Show Biz, knowing that your wife was somewhere on an upper floor, unconscious, while part of her breast was being removed to be scientifically decimated.

Mr Whitton and his Harrods/Savile Row suit approached. Robin was numb.

"It was cancer," said Mr Whitton. "I have removed her breast."

What do you say in response to a man who tells you that? wondered Robin. Do I say thank you? Hardly. Do I say no thank you? Hardly.

Robin was outside the recovery room when Gillian was wheeled out that day. Don't cry, he told himself.

Gillian won't cry. Gillian was strong. Stronger than me, thought Robin. Don't cry. The tears gushed from his eyes.

"You look awful." Gillian spoke slowly. "I should get up and you should lie down." Robin tried to laugh.

In the elevator going down to her room, she opened her eyes briefly. Robin, the drips and tubes to one side, held her hand tightly.

"Am I dying?" she asked simply.

"No," Robin assured her, "you're not dying."

"Good, then take care of me," she struggled to say. Robin nodded. "If you can't, I can't," she said.

"It'll be okay, kid," said Robin, "you'll be okay." She squeezed his hand. "You can. I can," he said.

She closed her eyes. And smiled.

Robin knew then that one day Gillian would find a way to have her body reshaped.

CHAPTER

11

"I'm not going to have a bypass," Peter declared, looking out of the window onto the dirty brick wall opposite. If this is a private room, Robin thought, I expect in the public wards to find Mr Charles Dickens. Silk pyjamas from Jermyn Street and an initialled towel robe, probably Christmas gifts from Millicent, replaced Peter's previous hospital attire, helping break the dinginess of the Victorian surrounds.

"Mr Andersen, you should be in bed," a nurse admonished as she entered the room.

"I should be in a lot of things," replied Peter, "including in you." But he meekly returned to the bed. It was a sign of the new Peter; the Peter of only days ago would not have yielded so easily.

As the nurse tucked him in, the old Peter, as if reading Robin's mind, re-emerged. "How about a little grope of your ass?" he asked.

"Mr Andersen, stop it!" She pushed his poised hand away. "You're too old."

"Thanks," Peter replied. And lowered his hand.

The nurse turned to Robin. "Your friend is—"

"Yes," said Peter, "aren't I?" The nurse left.

"They – the medics – keep chuntering on about a bypass." Peter lapsed into an imitation of a Harley Street voice: "'We strongly advise it, Mr Andersen. Strongly recommend . . .' Well, I'm not going to do it."

Robin waited.

"I *am* going to change," said Peter. "I'll eat all that crap. All that yuk. Potatoes and baked beans. Cereals and pulses. What a poxy name! Pulses. Poxy pustules of pulses for puking. Now there's a phrase. Try it at the office . . . And I'll cut out the fat. Goodbye steaks rump, steaks fillet, steaks tartare – ta-ta to tartare. I'll be a good little lad. And I'm to cut down on the booze. Just a glass every now and then, for medicinal purposes. Don't say what kind of glass, do they? One of those old balloons, mebbe . . ." He paused to take a deep breath. "And I must exercise. Gently. My father used to say there's only one exercise for a gentleman . . . No. That's what I would've wanted my father to say . . ."

Peter's voice trailed off.

"Can I have first refusal on the Andersen wine cellar?" asked Robin.

Peter smiled. "And I'm leaving the shop. It's all yours," he said.

Robin nodded. Provision had been made when the partnership was first formed for illness overtaking one or both of them.

"You'll stay on as a consultant," said Robin. It was a small bone to the dog called vanity. And both knew it.

"Consultant? Of course," said Peter, "I'd be delighted."

Robin stood. The partners shook hands.

"One thing I won't cut down on," Peter said, "cunt. Any I can get, I'm there. No matter where. No matter how many. Let's make a bet. How many women d'y'think I can screw before this," he tapped his heart, "packs up? A hundred? Two? Three? Bet it's more like five hundred. Think of it, five hundred lovely koozies just waiting for me."

"You'll wear a condom, of course," said Robin drily.

Peter laughed. "Get Gillian to make me a bread and butter pudding. She makes the best bread and butter pudding in London. No, in ... Wait. Am I allowed to eat butter?"

"No," said Robin, "Gillian will make you a bread-substitute and butter-substitute pudding."

"Did I ever tell you how much I hate ties?" asked Peter.

"No. Never."

"I'll get Millie to go along and empty my wardrobe.

My office uniforms. All those suits. And shirts. And ties. You can keep the ties."

"Gosh, even the kipper ones?" said Robin.

The friends said goodbye to each other.

CHAPTER

12

The noise from the Paris streets had not abated. Robin knew that Clara was not sleeping. He was wide awake. They lay side by side on their backs, eyes closed, under the thinnest sheet to be found.

Each time Robin stretched his hand towards Clara, rested it on her hip, her breathing stopped. Her fear was almost tangible. But was it fear? Or excitement? He tried again. This time she intercepted his hand with hers.

I can't, he thought. I don't believe this, he said to himself. This can't be. I'm lying next to this beautiful woman and I know what's going to happen. Nothing. Nothing's going to happen. I'm not going to do it. I'm not going to fuck her. I must. I'll throw the sheet off and tear through her clothes and do it ... I can't, he thought, I can't, I can't.

He got out of bed, softly cursed her baggage for

hurting his toe, and searched for the Perrier bottle delivered so many hours earlier. The liquid was warm. But he poured the bubbling water into his glass. Turned. And trod on a buckle of her suitcase. This time he swore loudly.

Clara sat up. "Are you all right?" she asked. "You drink too much."

"Don't tell me what to do," he said sharply.

A slight exhalation came from her at the abruptness of his reply.

Robin was delighted with his anger. Maybe that's what it needs, anger, to force her to my will. Get angrier, go on, rage and roar. Let passion swell to uncontrollable heights.

He went round to her side of the bed. And sat facing her. She pulled the sheet to her.

"It's not whisky, it's water," Robin explained. "Do you want a sip?"

She leaned forward for her lips to find the glass in his hand. He looked down on the back of her head. The only lighting in the room came from the street, floors below. His free hand caressed the back of her hair. She sat back immediately. Tired eyes glared at him. "Tell me about your wife," she asked.

Robin sensed she was referring more to Gillian's illness than to knowing about Gillian. "Ten years ago she had a mastectomy," he replied. Clara gasped. Robin waited, then continued, "Eight years ago she had a reconstruction. Then she was okay, well, almost okay. Last year, it came back. Hot spots. On her bones. She lost weight. She lost height. Then remission, and she was okay again, not herself, but okay." Why, Robin mused as he spoke, did dialogue become simpler and words more monosyllabic as one became drunker? "Then last month, she—" He tried to go on, but found he couldn't. The whisky regurgitated back into his throat, mingling with hidden tears. He felt nauseous.

Neither of them spoke for some time. What a ludicrous picture, thought Robin, both of us half-dressed, sitting on the edge of a bed in the middle of a steamy night in Paris, not talking, not touching, nothing. Clara leaned forward, her hand rested lightly on his two fingers closest to her.

"I'm sorry," she said, "so sorry. For both of you."

Robin nodded. Her body outlined itself beneath the sometimes clinging, sometimes loose pyjamas, etching its form into his imagination. I should rape her, he thought. Pull off those pyjamas, rape her. She would never charge me, wouldn't have me arrested, never. Not the sort. Go on, do it. Take what you want. Rape.

He recalled Peter's voice over some distant pub drink. "Women are terrified of rape. If they knew how much the thoughts of men were obsessed with sex, they would really have cause to be frightened."

Robin had shrugged and replied, "I admit I think about sex a lot. Can't remember any rape though." Ah

Peter, Peter, what would you do in this situation? "Not every man can rape," he had replied.

"Yes, he can. Any man can," declared Peter. "Even you."

"What's your wife's name?" asked Clara suddenly.

"Worry ye not," he replied.

"What?" she said.

"Worry ye not. It's a phrase I picked up." Clara looked at him quizzically. He decided not to tell her Gillian's name. That was too much betrayal. All right to talk of mastectomies and hot spots but naming names was bringing the marriage into this tiny bedroom. "Go to sleep," he said, rising.

He went into the bathroom, ran tepid water from the cold tap over his wrists, splashed his face, did not dare to look at himself in the mirror. By the time he returned to bed, Clara was breathing more evenly in some sort of sleep. Should I try just once more? he wondered. No. I can't. Admit it, at least to yourself. You can't do it. Not you. Not you.

He rolled onto his side and begged sleep to overwhelm him. Eventually his pleas were answered.

CHAPTER

13

"A few loose cells behind the eyes, that's all," Professor Knights said.

"Is it cancerous?" Gillian asked. "It's all right, you can tell me."

Professor Knights issued a tolerant smile. "Possibly," he said, "probably. But if it is cancer, this time we can contain it. With radiotherapy." He picked up the phone and asked a member of the radiotherapy department, Dr McDonnell, to join them as soon as possible.

"Where are you going for your holidays?" asked Knights. The standard June question. He described his own intentions, to camp out in the far north of Scotland with a wife and five extremely small children, fishing. "Do you fish?" he asked.

"Never caught a thing," answered Robin, conscious

only of Gillian shifting about uneasily. "Much to the disgust of my father."

"Well, you should try—"

"Does that mean the remission is over?" Gillian cut across the banter.

Knights shrugged. "I don't think so. A few rogue cells. That's all."

Dr McDonnell entered the room. A small man with a high nasal voice, thinning hair, and spoiled-child manner, he was forever dressed in a blue blazer and dark grey trousers, disdaining the hospital smocks worn by other doctors in order to proclaim his own sartorial values. The blazer and slacks constantly appeared in need of another visit to the cleaners.

The two doctors squared up to each other. The enmity between them was covered by a veneer of politeness. Dr McDonnell did not appear to think much of Professor Knights, who had a superior role in the oncology section of the hospital, although to their credit both seemed determined not to let it affect any patient's well-being. Nevertheless the tension was there.

When parking the car, and looking back over her shoulder, Gillian had become aware of double vision in her left eye. She had told Robin. Hence the return to the hospital.

The two cancer doctors left Gillian and Robin sitting in the office while they went into the bustling corridor to confer.

Gillian took both Robin's hands in hers. "Eight months. Not long, is it? Eight months," she said, continually twisting Robin's hands between hers. Was she going to break now? Instead, she said, "I'm not going to die of cancer, y'know."

"Of course not," he said.

"I'm not," she continued. "I'll die being killed by a bus. I will, a bus, not cancer ... Don't worry, for you I'll make sure it's the right kind. Red bus, double decker."

Eight. No one ever talks of eight as a magic number. Seven. Eleven. Thirteen. Six six six. Never eight. Oh yes, the Chinese. And Gillian's count of eight months of remission was accurate. And it was eight years after the cancer was first diagnosed that it had returned to enshroud the days of Gillian and Robin again. Was eight their doom number?

Such were Robin's thoughts as once more he dodged the car past the inevitable roadworks, towards Hammersmith Broadway, stopping, starting, braking, lurching, minimal movements forward followed by much waiting until another minimal movement allowed him to advance a few inches. Gillian was left behind in the hospital. For another blood transfusion and an early morning start at zapping "those few cells". Robin glanced at his watch. His flowers would have arrived by now. The nurses on the fifteenth floor – eight plus seven? doesn't fit – would be scattered by Gillian once again to search for an extra two or three vases. How long, dear God, can this go on? How many more rooms? How many more flowers? And needles, and injections, and blood bags, and saline drips? And blue pills plus pink pills but no yellow pills until bedtime, please note, but the brown pills every two hours, okay? A rainbow of medication. And the names, the many new names, to be sorted, isolated, separated in order to acknowledge each had a different function, a different usage, and regrettably, different side effects. Morphine, Temazapam, Didronel, Co-amilozide, Co-danthramer, Navidrex, and Motillium – let's not forget Motillium that stops you from puking up all the others. Names that ranged from A for Aspav to Z for Zantac. Will I ever learn them all? Whatever happened to aspirin and penicillin? And my emotions, like bloodhounds around a fox, being gouged apart. And what about her? What about my wife, a woman called Gillian, in a room she hates in a building called a hospital, literally being rendered asunder by a devouring disease? For how much longer, sweet Jesus, how much longer? And Robin knew the answer. For as long as it takes, was the only answer. Don't let her die, he prayed, please God, don't. Crippled she is, no more my beautiful woman, but please, let her live. Let me die first, please, dear God, I beg you.

Pedestrians easily outpaced the cars creeping into the Broadway. Robin put the gear into neutral. And did the same with his thoughts. What the hell is this sudden calling on the deity? he asked himself. And smiled. Scenes of the debating hall at Princeton appeared on the screen of his imagination. "An atheist should always have the right to say 'God damn it, I'm an atheist.' First speaker to defend this proposition, Robin Laurent Jr." He lost the debate. You either believe in a supreme power or you don't, ruled the student body. Quite right, he thought then. Quite right, he thought now. Throughout her life Gillian had also scorned the mumbo-jumbo, and the comfort, of religion. She was typically of this country, he thought, tolerant of anyone else's beliefs as long as they left her free to believe what she wanted. And seeing no contradiction in the fact that she knew the church's hymns – at least the good ones – so well. She would sing lustily, heartily at funerals and weddings and christenings, the only time they stepped onto holy ground, over-paying for the privilege with large contributions onto the passing plate. All Things Bright and Beautiful, thought Robin, but not here in Hammersmith with the belch of cars stinking into his nose and mouth.

Recently Gillian had taken to meditation. In this she did find comfort. Earphones conveying messages from portable cassettes glided her away to more lyrical worlds, helping her to become tranquil, to rest, and, she believed, helping her immune system fight the disease. Murmurings from the neighbouring pillow were no longer muted love calls from his wife but the distorted mechanical voices of solace leaking from her headset. Gillian never troubled to tell Robin the contents of these cassettes. But like the books on the shelf – *You Can Conquer Cancer* and *Love, Medicine and Miracles* – their numbers increased. Well-meaning friends also proffered well-meaning advice. "The grape diet," said Millicent, "eat nothing but grapes. It worked for this woman who ..." Gillian tried it for three days. "I'm beginning to hate grapes," she said finally, "even seedless ones." The grape cure was abandoned.

Crystals. All sorts of crystals, both rough and polished, began to appear on her dressing table, among the make-up pots that she now used less and less.

"Hold this," she turned from the table one night to hand Robin a large new acquisition of crystal, "millions and millions of years old."

"Good to know there's something older than me."

"Can't you feel it?" She took it back and cupped the stone in both hands. "It has warmth. Character. Almost a life of its own."

Autogenic training and psychotherapy were part of Gillian's life from the earliest days of the disease. Counselling and reading, especially the reading of philosophy, were expanding activities with the first diagnosis. She enrolled in the Open University, determined to get a degree but mainly to help discipline her approach to the philosophers. Textbooks were bought, never borrowed; Gillian couldn't bear to read a book unless she owned it. Loose-leaf notebooks. Extra tapes to record the lectures off the television. Pencils. Pens. Crammers. A student, again.

"I'm going to be as smart as you," she told Robin.

"You'll never be that smart," he replied. "But you will be educated."

In her second year, having finally left the Greek thinkers behind, Robin returned late one night to find her in bed, glasses on, table lamp burning, surrounded by large books. "Who is it this year?" he asked.

"Your wife is in bed with two gentlemen, well, men anyway, called Hobbes and Kant," she said.

"Two boring old farts," said Robin. "When you get to Spinoza, tell me."

She did. And they would argue endlessly about the Dutchman's philosophy, agreeing and disagreeing with him, with each other, talking constantly while taking the children on the school run or in the garden clearing leaves or while she cooked, vehemently shaking a pepper mill for emphasis.

"This is serious," said Robin. "If Baruch Spinoza is responsible for your ruining the Cod Portuguese, I'll never forgive him."

Then one night, Michael in bed asleep, Samuel upstairs in front of a muted television, both sat reading before the fire, a scene of cosy domesticity shattered when she leaped up and ran for the bathroom. Robin followed. And found her sobbing. Gillian, who cried so infrequently, threw herself into his arms.

"He – Baruch – he's been excommunicated – if that's the word – banished from the synagogue for his writing. How could that happen?"

"It happens." He held her tight. "'Such men are dangerous. They think too much.' His thinking didn't fit. And at that time—"

"But he was so religious. God, God, always God with him," she said. "They made him lie down at the door of the temple and the entire community, one by one, stepped over him. His pain, the anguish. Why do we do that to each other?" She glanced at herself in the mirror. "Gawwwd, look at me! Eyes running, make-up running." She started to fix herself. "I hate to think what'll happen when I get to the Tolpuddle Martyrs!"

It had been more than five minutes since any car moved. Robin saw an opening leading to the Odeon cinema. And took it. He parked the car and walked along the riverside to The Doves. He decided against drinking since he was certain to be called back to the hospital and sat sombrely sipping mineral water among the early evening revellers, staring at the Thames and its murky, forbidding waters rushing towards Hammersmith Bridge. Not the prettiest bridge in the world. And certainly not the most dramatic. But containable. Homely. A typical London bridge.

Why would the God of Baruch Spinoza or the God of anybody want to torture Gillian so? To keep offering her the hope of further life and then snatching it away? Psychology to help her mentally. Chemotherapy to help her physically. Remission to say the disease has stopped. Remission-over to say the cancer has returned. Up. And down. The roller-coaster ride to recovery. Torture.

From the next table came a loud burst of laughter. Laughter? Do people still laugh? A group of eight or nine young men and women jammed around a sodden and glass-laden table next to Robin. One of the girls, pretty in an indefinite manner, smiled at him as if to apologize for the disturbance. He nodded back. Whereupon one of the men, plump, shirted belly protruding over his belt — why is it always the least attractive? — having seen this exchange between Robin and the girl, tilted his head back to roar another echoing laugh. Like a bull moose establishing his male prerogatives. The bull's laugh provoked more titters from the ensemble. Good. Laugh, kids, laugh. Enjoy it while you can. If there is a God then He's a cruel bastard, giving us so much, including summer evenings by the Thames in joyous company, and laughter and women and flirting and fucking, all of this thing called life are we given, then after a miserly three score and ten, He takes it all away.

Robin tried to discipline his thinking. Trace it all, clearly, he told himself, from the beginning. Eight years after the original diagnosis, after the mastectomy, after being told the disease may never return and after her insisting she live at least ten more years, eight years later Gillian complained of being unable to write her university essays. Osteoporosis. That was the diagnosis this time. One specialist after another told her about the deterioration of bone tissue as one gets older. This time Robin had let her do the Harley Street search on her own. Until Millicent cornered him at the office one day. "Something's wrong," she said, "she's with you every day. You can't see it. I can." Robin took Gillian back to Mr Whitton. For X-rays and a body scan. Hot spots. Mr Whitton pointed out the discovered hot spots. The disease had metastasized — a new word to be added to the family lexicon — into her bones.

And so began the familiarity with Charing Cross hospital. Nooks and crannies, corridors and rooms unknown even to staff members became commonplace to Robin and Gillian. Procedures were established. The rituals of Monday morning. First, on the scales to be weighed. Then into the loo to leave some urine. On to the blood room. A problem for Gillian here. Small veins meant difficulty in extracting blood. Until an older nurse suggested dipping her forearm in hot water first. Then the waiting. Endless waiting. Forever waiting. Robin and Gillian always had plenty to talk about and could never understand other couples who sat in restaurants, for instance, wordlessly staring at each other. Even at home there were always plenty of thoughts and information and events to be related, unlike others to whom talk across the dining table or the bathroom basin was a rarity. But hospital waiting rooms are not conducive to conversation. A lack of privacy. Or the anticipation of something fearful. Or unconsciously knowing this to be a vacuum, away from life, and therefore devoid of simple things like words. Gillian would sit and watch others, the patients, the nurses, the doctors to-ing and fro-ing. Robin read newspapers. Until summoned into the sanctum of the professor's office. Gillian had insisted on reserving the first appointment of the day at 8.30 a.m. but rarely achieved it. Chronic cases or doctors demanding the professor's urgent attention displaced her allotted time. Gillian was patient. Robin was determined not to show his impatience to her.

The ritual of Wednesday mornings concerned radio-therapy. Gillian was led into a cubicle, remarkably resembling a padded cell as if she were some mediaeval madwoman needing to be isolated to be cured, where gamma rays bombarded first her hips and later her ribs and sternum. She never complained. Robin could only watch and admire and feel totally incapable of helping the woman he married. Except for the occasional embrace of comfort.

Radiotherapy gave way to chemotherapy. And finding

the Chinese doctor. And meditation. And crystals. And acupuncture. And reflexology. And many, many books. So the spring months passed.

Gillian began to lose weight and height. Not all at once. But the unrelenting progress of the illness was soon marked. Robin induced her to go to the south of France for a week. "Do us both good," he insisted. She shrugged and eventually agreed. She was eating so little. He thought the arrays of tantalizing food might stimulate her appetite.

They returned to the Colombe d'Or in St Paul de Vence where smiling staff — 'biensûr' — said they remembered them from their honeymoon. Robin took this to be politic: Gillian did not look much like her former self. When she ate so little, waiters swarmed at the table and with much tut-tutting and shaking of heads tried to cajole her into eating. But she could not.

One day as Robin sat by the pool reading, Gillian, who spent most of her waking hours sleeping and most of her sleeping hours sleeping, appeared beside him dressed for a swim. This surprised Robin for she no longer showed her body in public. A long robe shielded her from head to toe until the moment when she could slip into the water. She stood, pushed hair under her bathing cap, and asked casually, "Am I dying, Robin?"

He could only guess at what had gone on in the hotel room. Had she stood in front of those long amber mirrors surveying herself? She would have seen the loosened skin, the widow's stoop increasing too rapidly as if age were accelerating towards her uncontrollably. "Am I dying, Robin?" she repeated.

The medical profession had anticipated this moment. "Your wife will one day ask you this question," the family physician Dr Lundt had warned, "and you must, after comforting her, tell her the truth. If you lie, and tell her she's not dying, she will never trust you again. She must be able to rely on you for the truth. Not platitudes."

"We are all dying," said Robin, aware of how platitudinous he was being.

"Stop that!" she said sharply. "Well?" She looked at him steadily.

"Gillian, I—" he started. "Yes, my darling, I think you are."

Gillian exhaled visibly. She looked as if he had just kicked her in the stomach. "You think I'm dying! You think I'm dying! I'm not! I'm not! I knew it, how dare you think that? Gawdammit, I'm not." He put his arms around her to try and stop the flow of wrath. "You want me to die, is that it?"

"Gillian, please," he pleaded as she pulled away.

She removed the bathing cap and threw it at him. Followed by the towel, his book, papers, magazines, cushions and anything else she could find.

In a cloud of fury she headed back to the hotel but turned in the doorway to shout back at him, "You don't think I can do it, do you? Well, I can! I can! I can beat it. I'll do it without you. Damn you! I'll do it alone!"

All those at the pool both in and out of the water had stopped to watch this domestic sideshow. Robin closed in on Gillian and tried to take her in his arms. She pushed him away. "You don't love me. You never have loved me!" She rushed into the hotel. Robin sheepishly gathered their belongings. And followed.

He had to knock at their door several times before she answered. "Go away," she said finally. "Find yourself some French bit. Leave me alone."

At the bar, cuddling a large glass of Macallan, Robin glanced at his watch. Manny Margolis would be with his first patient of the day, Robin calculated, noting the time difference, but maybe he could sneak away for a quick talk. Robin found a phone and rang New Jersey. "It's called denial," said Manny's warm baritone voice over the transatlantic phone, "and some people go on denying right up to the last moment. And the only way to help them is to deny with them. Knowing Gillian, how strong she is, I think she'll refuse to recognize dying until about eight seconds before she goes. If then." Manny Margolis was an old friend, going back as far as pre-Princeton days at Kleber High, who was now a professor of psychiatry as well as heading the department at Cedars Sinai Hospital. Robin had consulted him on medical matters before this. "What your doctor was saying — and he should've known better — is that a number of people deny, deny, deny that they're dying, until there comes a moment when they want to be told, usually by a loved one, the truth. And they draw strength from that. Knowing there's someone by their side they can trust from that moment on. But that won't apply with Gillian. Each case is different. Gillian's strong because she denies. It helps her. She wants you to deny with her. That'll give her strength. So no matter what you're thinking about her condition worsening, keep it to yourself, and you'll help her to live longer." The phone went silent for a moment. "Y'know, Robin, she'll probably outlive you." Robin said amen to that and after a few pleasantries about the psychiatrist's wife, children and other friends, was about to hang up when Manny added, "If Gillian wants to live, she'll live. You've got to believe that. She does."

When the room service waiter put the gin and tonic down in front of her, Gillian protested volubly. Alcoholic drinks do not mix with morphine. An occasional minute sip of Robin's wine was all she allowed herself. But Robin knew how much she missed her favourite cocktail. And encouraged her to drink as much as she dared while he told her about his conversation with Manny, edited slightly so as not to mention the word denial and to highlight Manny's conviction that Gillian could and would conquer the disease. And that he, Robin, was wrong ever to think otherwise.

"I'm sorry," Robin said. "I wish I could take back

this afternoon. I don't know what got into me." He did not mention Dr Lundt and the faulty advice.

"You're under a strain," she said. "I'm sick. It shows on me. And it shows in you."

He took both her hands in his. "Don't ever doubt that I love you."

"I don't."

"If I could have the disease for you, I would. That's not just words. I mean it."

She touched his face. Seemed to struggle to speak, swallowed a few times. And then said softly, "I know. And it's wonderful knowing that. It helps me. More than I can say ..." She abruptly changed the subject and that was the moment the red bus theory was born. "But I'm not going to die of cancer. It'll be a bus, double decker. Do they run down Bond Street? No? I'll have to arrange it in front of Harrods then."

Strangely enough Gillian ate quite a reasonable meal that evening.

CHAPTER

14

If a butterfly lands on our windows, Robin hears it. A quote from Gillian. Aeons ago. At some dinner party. Gillian explaining how Robin's pattern had changed from the selfish deep sleep of bachelorhood to ever-alert parental sleep. The lion in the den wakening when the jungle sounds come too close. Even if the threatening predator is only a butterfly.

Clara was in the bathroom, making noises stealth made even louder. A jar, a glass, a pot, clinking against tiles. Trying to be quiet. Not succeeding.

"*Est-ce qu'il est possible*—" Robin phoned the concierge who assured him it would be possible to get some cold water.

"Did I wake you? Sorry. Sorry," said Clara opening the bathroom door, speaking nervously, clipped phrases to avoid lengthy conversation. "I need something for my tum. That fish, I think. Maalox or Pepto—"

"Be different brand names. But the same stuff." Robin squeezed past her to find his medicine bag. "Nothing wrong with that fish." He held out a handful of antacids.

Clara seemed to regard the unfamiliar packaging with some suspicion. "Well," she said, "maybe you're right, maybe I don't need them. Sorry I woke you. You've only had about an hour …"

A knock on the door. The sweating concierge handed over two large bottles, one plain, one carbonated. And, wonder of wonders, a small glass bucket of ice. "*Eh, voilà,*" said the concierge, smiling. Robin tipped him profusely in both words and money.

Clara pounced on the ice. The top buttons of her pyjamas were undone for the first time. Her front was open down to a shadowy cleavage. Her neck was wet. Using a small handkerchief she had mopped her neck in the bathroom. Now she took two ice cubes and carefully positioned them in the cloth. Robin watched a drip of water snake its way down towards her bosom.

"Plain or fizz?" he asked.

"Fizzy," she replied.

Gassy water bubbled over the ice. They stood close to each other sharing the same glass. Back and forth. She drank. He drank. Lips at first avoiding where the other one drank, then not caring. He could feel the heat from her body. She must feel his. The smell of her filled his nostrils. He was suffocating with her odours. And the heat of the night. The heat of the room. Heat. The glass refilled. Drinking. The relief of cold water.

She held the handkerchief to the back of her neck. And shivered slightly. Was it the ice?

Clara moved to the bed, sat down. As she did so an ice cube fell out of the handkerchief, down her front. Instinctively she leaned forward, pulled her clothing away, revealing her breasts, glistening, wet. She glanced up fearfully at Robin, then quickly tried to cover herself.

In an instant he was beside her. Buttons popped through the air. The torn top came apart surprisingly quickly in his hands. And the struggles of her sweating body seemed only to help the removal of the pyjama bottoms as he tore and pulled them away. He stood before her holding her clothing. She was naked.

She cowered away. Up the bed. Pulling at the sheet as she retreated. Robin held the sheet back.

She was at the head of the bed, her legs tucked under her, reminiscent of her position just before dinner.

But this time she was naked.

The glory of the female form, from which his eyes had been deprived for so long, seemed more wondrous than ever. The curves, the roundness, the skin, the colour, the hair, the shadows, all were before him. But, ah, the breasts. Once his eyes saw her breasts, he could see nothing else. And her nipples, pink, rosy, alluring, were compelling him forward.

He stepped towards her.

"No. Don't." She began to cry. "Don't."

What does she really want me to do? Please. Help me. What does she want? What do I want? I must not stop. I must stop. His thoughts ached with indecision. His eyes were still locked on to her breasts.

Clara took advantage of his mesmerization to jump towards the bathroom. Once she was alongside him, he grabbed her arm, tightly, and she could not move. She looked up at him. Tears filled her eyes. She shook her head, hesitantly, pleading.

Robin slowly extended his free hand and tenderly cupped her breast. She put her head back, trembled.

He looked into her eyes for some time. He did not want to release her. He wanted to hold this breast. To hold this woman. He wanted this moment to go on. And on. Forever. But he let her go.

As he stepped onto the small veranda he could hear the bathroom door shut. The whisky bottle was with him. He tilted it towards his lips, changed his mind. He was tired. Needed to sleep. He was sweating. He wanted to be cool. Most of all he needed to think. Not drink.

CHAPTER

15

"Y' got no gumption, boy!" His father's hand and arm could move at incredible speed. Whiplash. The hand always caught the back of Robin's head, near the crown, flicking it abruptly down and forward. Painful. Robin was never spanked. No need. This was a much more formidable form of punishment. To be exercised by the senior Laurent at will. On winter nights, in front of the fire, while holding a book in his other hand. Flick. Summer days, as Robin ran past the porch. Flick. Never a warning. Sometimes with an open hand. More often a closed fist. More painful. Never a reason given. Sometimes it was justified. Often not.

"I send y' for a chicken," said the father, "and y' come back with nothin'." The first Sunday of every month. A ritual. A chicken for Sunday lunch. Chickens were housed in the shed, coop, down at the wilder part of the garden. A good year saw twenty or more birds. A bad year, five or six. The family would return from church. The girls upstairs to change. Mother aproning herself in the kitchen. Robin dispatched to select the doomed animal.

The squawk of death. The cries of fear. It was as if the chickens knew. Or so it seemed to seven-year-old Robin as he entered the shed. The sound of anticipated slaughter. Loud, piercing into one ear before megaphoning out of the other. Fear. He would never forget that sound. Which one shall it be? Which one shall be condemned to the dining table? That one! I'm sorry, you are going to die. Sorry. No? Then that one! He chases one bird. Changes his mind. Tries another. Hands to his head all the while to keep the horror out of his ears. The chickens scatter. The cacophony grows. Robin is crying. Finally, head on chest, eyes wiped to hide his tears, he exits from the shed, walks slowly down the path to face his father.

"Y're useless, boy!" Flick. Robin Senior grabs his son's arm and half lifts the boy back towards the shed. The chicken screams return. "Pick one!" shouts the father above the din. Robin shakes his head. An ache filling his chest prevents him from speaking. Flick. "I said pick one!" Another shake of the head. Crying. Flick. Then flick, flick, flick. Still the little head shakes. Fed up, the father ignores the leghook and easily catches a rounded fowl, expertly tests it for plumpness by

squeezing the breast, jams the bird into Robin's hands.
Flick. "Useless." Flick. "Don't lose it!" Robin holds the
squawking chicken by the legs, as terrified of letting go
as the bird is of its forthcoming fate.

At the lunch table, Robin Senior sees that his son
is not eating the chicken. "Eat it." The boy raises his
eyes. The always-aching chest has killed all desire for
food. But he knows not to argue. A morsel slips into
his mouth. Chews. Slowly. Water, drink lots of water,
he tells himself. "More." When the boy hesitates, the
father's fork tears off a huge piece of chicken. "Robin!"
says the mother from the other end of the table. Why is
she such a shadow in all this? Why didn't she intervene?
Was she as afraid of him as I was? These questions came
to him years later. His sisters, too young or too wise, did
not appear to notice. "Stay out o' it," his father warns his
mother. Cupping his son's face open with his free hand,
the father pushes the chicken into the boy's mouth. Less
than a minute later, despite lashings of water, Robin tries
to leave the table. "Where y'goin', boy?" The father stops
his son. Mistake. The uncontrollable speed at which the
half-chewed food spewed out of Robin's mouth, amazed
them both. All over the father's Sunday shirt, tie and
trousers.

Robin was never forced to eat chicken again.

Shortly after this Robin learned not to cry at the head
cuffing. No matter how painful, he held his tears. His
father soon tired of it. The flicking stopped.

And subsequently in Robin's worldly travels, chicken bonne femme or chicken cacciatori or chicken veronique or chicken and forty cloves of garlic or chicken romana or coq au vin or chicken soup or Cornish hens or corn-fed chickens or free-range chickens or chicken in aspic or chicken and almonds or chicken Kiev or chicken koftas or devilled chicken or curried chicken or plain old roasted chicken or indeed any of the other many chicken dishes, could never disguise the taste of that chicken that Sunday morning. Chicken was not his favourite dish.

CHAPTER

16

The lights from the bridge and the shore opposite were reflected strongly in the darkening waters. Robin sat, still nurturing bottles of mineral water, his chair eyed covetously by standing patrons of the now over-crowded pub.

He had phoned the hospital earlier. Gillian beseeched him not to return. But he insisted and said he would be with her in an hour. I'd better eat, he thought. Among the minimally lit interior bars he found the food counter. The display was headlined by cottage pie, steak-and-kidney pie and spaghetti bolognese. Rubbish. At least in Robin's opinion, spoiled by years of Gillian's cooking. The equivalent back home of spicy chicken wings, barbecued ribs and hamburgers. Garbage. Which was the more boring, he mused for a moment, this country's junk food or his country's junk food. He decided on cottage pie – meat loaf with potatoes to him – and returned to the patio. His seat was long gone. So he stood, plate on the railing, to eat his dinner.

When he and Gillian returned from the Côte d'Azur – nobody calls it that any more, do they? – she switched from philosophy to Greek and Roman history at the Open University. She continued her medication which she administered to herself. One blue morphine tablet in the morning. One pink morphine tablet at night. A motillium to stop any nausea. A Zantac to settle her stomach. Two aspirin substitutes twice a day. Hospital treatment, radiotherapy and chemotherapy, appeared to be a thing of the past, although she and Robin were called on to report to various departments once a fortnight.

Robin found the expected solace in his work. Then came the day when his secretary Marilyn, knowing that Gillian never called unless it was of consequence, interrupted a board meeting to whisper as undramatically as she could, that his wife was on the line. It was later that day Robin and Gillian sat like communicants in front of the priest, Professor Knights. Remission. Granted for good behaviour. Perhaps even for bad behaviour. But granted nevertheless. Remission.

What a soft word. A gentle word. A blessed word.

"Let's take a chance on Portugal," Gillian said one day. She had returned from a favourite pastime, shopping on the High Street, and spread plastic bags from

Marks & Spencer, from the greengrocer, the butcher, fishmonger, newsagent, baker and many, many others over the kitchen table. "You love it," she said, "so do the boys." Three weeks was deemed to be enough. Unbeknown to Gillian, Robin steered the selection of the villa, with a few discreet calls to the letting agents, to one with no stairs.

It was only seconds after the family arrived at the villa before Samuel and Michael left a trail of clothing on the terracotta tiles as they stripped and plunged into the pool, rejoicing in the heat and emancipation a warmer climate brings. The house, high on the Cerra d'Agua — crest of the eagle — overlooked beaches from the poolside, while miles of verdant vineyards and olive groves could be seen from the bedrooms. Robin and his sons spent hours on the beach; swimming, windsurfing, hiring the occasional power boat or motor scooter, but most of all snorkelling. Even the grasshopper needs of a pre-teenager like Michael were tranquillized floating around rocks' edges following a school of minnows.

Gillian stayed at the villa. Robin ensured that either Lisa, the latest au pair girl who had travelled with them, or Maria, the in-every-way abundant Portuguese maid, were on hand in case needed by Gillian. One evening, several days after they arrived, Robin was mixing a gin and tonic, a drink he only tolerated in hot weather, when Gillian approached. "Can I have a sip?" she asked.

"I'll make you one," he said, somewhat surprised but

pleased, and immediately began to mix considerably less gin into a fresh drink.

"Let's go out tonight," said Gillian. Robin stared at his wife. In the past, at previous summer villas in whatever country, holidays meant freedom from the kitchen for Gillian, and evening meals either tested Robin's prowess at the barbecue or, more usually, meant exploratory visits to the best of local restaurants. The acceptance or rejection of a villa as being suitable or not could often depend – after Robin had lengthy conversations with the owner – on the number of outstanding restaurants near at hand. No villa was ever hired without knowing the best dining places in the area. But that was in the past. This year dinners had all been on the terrace and consisted of either Robin's cooking or Maria's heaped plates. Gillian seemed not to want to show herself in public.

For a change it took little to convince Samuel and Michael that night to dress in clean shirts and jeans. All eyes in the restaurant, L'Atlantico in Pera, a typical white-based warm-country eating place, seemed to turn to look at two handsome boys and a frail, stooped woman, clearly old before her time, leaning heavily on her husband's arm, being shown to a table.

Once seated, as the menus were being handed over, Robin caught Samuel's eyes which his son quickly cast downwards. The boy was fighting to control himself. Was he remembering? Robin wondered.

"Why do people stare at us?" Samuel had asked that question two, maybe three, years ago — my God, was that all it was — after the foursome had entered some fashionable London restaurant.

"People do stare at other people coming into a restaurant," Robin had explained, "and besides, we're a good-looking lot."

"No, you're good-looking, I'm beautiful," said Gillian.

Then began choruses of "Oh no she's not!" and "Oh yes she is!" in the manner of children shouting at the stage at a Christmas pantomime until the giggling was subdued by an approaching waiter with an order book.

Two or three years ago. Now people stare at us for a different reason. But when Robin looked across the table again he saw Samuel take his mother's hand and squeeze it gently.

Through the glass panel of the hospital room's door, Robin could see the lights were still on above Gillian's head. But she was asleep. Surrounded by newspapers and magazines from which she had torn strips of printed columns and neatly stacked them to one side, mostly menus and cooking articles with one or two gardening items, while she lay amongst a pile of cushions. A blood bag was feeding her arm.

Robin stealthily removed the papers. Covered her.

Gillian did not move. A nurse came in, and after a mutual signal not to speak, dimmed the lights. Robin sat in the semi-darkness. And stared at his wife.

The summer tan was fading from Gillian's face.

After that first evening out, the holiday in Portugal changed somewhat. Gillian came to the beach once in a while. A parasol in the back row, as remote as possible from others, was always selected. As in France she was covered by a long robe, and when lying on the sun bed exposed mainly her face, sometimes her legs, nothing more. But Robin was comforted as he lay reading yesterday's newspaper — the most recent to be found abroad — that she was beside him.

She never went into the sea.

Her visits to the beach were rare. On a typical day she chose to go to San Rafael, her favourite place along the shore. Both children knew it well. "Has to be one of the best beaches in the world," said all-knowing twelve-year-old Michael waving an arm over the expanse of sand and rock as they arrived.

"Nah, not better than Coney Island," replied Gillian.

But the steep descent to the beach was difficult for her despite a railing and Robin's — or Samuel's — arm. And the return climb upwards was a trial. Robin could easily have carried her but knew she would refuse.

Lunch was taken at the beach bar. The boys would gorge themselves on the Iberian version of junk food, calamari and sardines and clams and chips and spaghetti

— "Spaghetti! What are the Portuguese doing making spaghetti?" "They have to because of the clientele." "Y'mean the Italians?" "No, the Germans" — while Robin and Gillian ate fish and salad.

After lunch the boys splashed into the water. Under the umbrella, Gillian slept. Robin watched the other bathers. The deep sandy beach was a haven for young families. Fathers of all shapes built castles of all sizes in the sand. Couples cuddled, families picnicked on coolboxes of food, people marched up and down the endless length of seashore.

One day, on the hardened foreshore near the water, Robin saw a game of beach tennis in progress. Two young women, topless, hit the ball, struggled to return it to two male opponents opposite. Robin could not take his eyes away. The girls ran, jumped, bounced, flounced, cavorted over the sand, splashed into the water, bumped into the occasional bystander. All this accompanied by a lot of laughter and a lot of shouting. But the breasts were all he saw. Oil-covered, sweaty, jiggling, bobbing, shaking, flapping, shimmering, bouncing, bouncing, bouncing firm breasts topped with red nipples overwhelmed in giant close-up the screen of his imagination. He watched. It was not erotic. Well, yes, it was. But it was more than erotic. It was an affirmation of life. An affirmation of the female body. Robin watched.

And thought of Gillian.

*   *   *

Snowflakes wafted down sparsely, dissolving when touching asphalt and pavement. Interlopers unwelcome on
city streets, the first harbingers of winter, skulking off
guiltily. It was cold. Too cold to snow. He stamped
repeatedly on the sidewalk. Cold feet, he said to himself,
in more ways than one. For the physical cold he knew
he should wear shoe coverings, galoshes and rubbers, as
he had in New Jersey but didn't dare in Manhattan.
Wrong image. For the other sort of cold feet, no ready
solution was available. It could be a mistake, he thought.
Big mistake. Though at the office water fountains and
at coffee, then over lunches, first in groups and then as
a twosome, always Dutch of course, she was fun to be
with, a ready laugh, easy to talk to and, most important,
a listener. So how bad can it be? As bad as some of
the others, he answered himself. A great city is a great
loneliness. Who said that? Must ask Dad. He needed a
companion. A female companion. Nothing serious. Just
once in a while. And if it became serious then it became
serious. What's wrong with that? Arguing with himself
he stood under the canopy of the Paris Cinema on West
60th Street waiting. Waiting for her.

Gillian arrived in a taxi.

Robin saw her pay off the driver. Turn. Apprehensive
eyes scanned the gathering number of cinemagoers, until

135

resting on Robin. Then a wave. And a smile. Her smile was doubly bright on a grey afternoon.

How appealing she looks, he thought to himself as he approached her. I must tell her. But instead, "You came in a cab," is what came out of his mouth. "How extravagant."

The smile diminished from her face. "Well, it's nice to see you too," was all she said.

"I earn a lot more than you." Why am I going on like this? he wondered. "And I came by subway."

"Bully for you," she said, "and how was it?"

"How was it? Cold and draughty and dirty and miserable. That's how it was. A subway."

"That's why I took a taxi." She tried to make light of it. "Besides, I like supporting all those Russians."

"What?"

"Every cabbie I get seems to be a Russian emigrant – immigrant. Aren't they?"

"Oh? Are they?"

He could almost hear her say to herself, this is going to be a long afternoon. He tried again.

"Taxis are a waste of money," he said.

She looked up at him. Anger flecked the corners of her eyes. "Last time I checked, your Hew Hess Hay was still a democracy. It's my money. I'll spend it how I like," she said.

The pause was awkward for both of them. This is the worst, he thought. Help. And I don't like her. How could I think I could ever like her? Feisty. Who needs a broad this feisty? He stamped his feet again, hunched his shoulders forward, trying to get warm. Her smile, locked into position, was now as cold as the weather.

She nodded towards the cinema doors. "Shall we go in, or do you want to go back to your delightful subway, while I waste more money on a taxi home?"

The film showing was a revival of *Some Like It Hot*. One lunchtime earlier that week, at a window table in the warm winter sun at Chasen's on 7th Avenue, Gillian confessed, "I've never seen it." Robin's lips narrowed in pretended terseness. "Smile when you say that, pardner," he said, "nobody uses low-down words in front of me and gets away with it." So the afternoon was arranged.

He did not hesitate in not taking her hand during the movie. Though he considered it. In the dark they sat. Apart. Side by side. But apart. Alone. Isolated. And determined to remain so. But the magic of Billy Wilder soon worked. Less than two hours later they emerged, warm from the glow of good entertainment, happy at having been transported out of themselves, still laughing. Instinctively she linked arms with him as they exited.

On the sidewalk outside the reality and the coldness returned. She self-consciously took her arm away. He let her do so.

"Well," she said.

"Well," he said.

It seemed to him she wanted to go. Yet she wanted to stay. What did he want? What should he do? One wrong word, he knew, and it would all be over. Finis. Was that what he wanted?

"Thank you for——" she started to speak.

"I thought——" he said.

The words overlapped. They stopped. She indicated that he should continue.

"Would you like to have tea?" He gestured towards the Plaza Hotel across the street. "I booked us a table. Wondered if you might like that. You being English an' all."

A beat. "How sweet," she said. "How thoughtful." She deliberately put her arm through his as they turned to cross the road.

"Shall we walk?" she asked mischievously. "Or take a taxi?"

A violin and a piano played melodies more suited to an older generation. Tea at the Palm Court. The bustle of genteel sounds. Muffled voices. In the foreground the music dominated. Gillian tried to remember various lyrics as she hummed and smattered along, chasing the more recognizable tunes.

"Yesterdays, yesterdays . . . sweet sequestered days . . ." She stopped. "What does that mean?" she asked. "I know it rhymes. Sort of. But what does it mean?"

"Sequester? I don't know."

"Yes, you do," she said. "Tell me."

"It's a legal term, isn't it?" he said. "Sequester. To remove, take away, set aside."

"What's it doing in a love song?" she wondered.

"I'll ask the President," he said.

Topics that might lead to fractioning were avoided. His work, her work, others at work — the bosses, Mr Kohler and Mr King, being given minute attention — all assayed to be safe, were discussed, if not over-discussed.

"Know any jokes?" she asked. "Sally Anne Willens — have you met Sally, my flatmate? — told me one." She took a deep breath. "It was a cold night in Mercy, Australia and this stranger was dying for a hot drink—" She started to laugh. Robin was never to hear another laugh like it. Infectious, nourishing, never mocking but rather life-giving, compelling anyone hearing it to join in. "So he goes into this pub and asks the publican, the barman, if he can have some hot tea because—" That's as far as she got. The laughter took over. "It's — it's — " she managed to squeeze out " — a great punch line."

Robin started to laugh. "Why am I laughing?" he asked. "I don't know this joke."

He couldn't help but laugh. And she couldn't finish the story; every time she tried, laughter forced her to stop. He reconciled himself to not hearing the end of the joke that night.

"About that argument earlier," he said. "Sorry. My fault."

She sipped tea. "What argument?"

"Outside the movie house, when I—" he started to say before realizing she was teasing. "Got me," he smiled.

"My fault too," she said.

"No, it wasn't. It was me."

"Well, it takes two to make an—"

He raised his voice in mock anger. "Are we going to argue now about whose fault it was?"

She laughed. "But it was my fault as well."

"Okay," he shrugged. "I admit it. It was you. It was your fault. All your fault."

"No, it wasn't," she said quickly, "you—" He started to laugh. After a moment she said, "Got me."

The music continued to envelop them.

"I wish we could dance," said Robin. "I want to hold you."

She leaned forward. "You don't need an excuse to hold me," she said. He took her hand.

They went by subway to arrive at the less pleasant parts of West 86th Street. Gillian had insisted. He wanted to go by taxi. "What, another argument?" he asked. But she knew he would never accept her offer to share the cost. So she suffered the subway.

On the doorstep she proffered her cheek to Robin while saying goodnight.

"Mona Lutzky told me—" she said.

"Mona who?"

"Mona Lutzky," said Gillian, "y'know, head of the

typing pool. Mona Lutzky tells me everything. All the rules. And Mona Lutzky says no kissing until the third date."

Robin laughed. But settled for kissing Gillian on the cheek before he left.

For their second date Robin selected one of the better Italian restaurants on West 57th Street. Then off to the theatre. To see *Follies*.

She conned him into letting her treat them to a drink in a bar round the corner. "Let me at least do that," she said.

"How did you find this place?" he asked as she sat, not unimpressed with the surroundings.

"Mona Lutzky," she replied. "Mona Lutzky—"

"—tells me everything," he finished the sentence for her.

"I liked that song," she said.

Robin checked the programme. "Y'mean 'In Buddy's Eyes'?"

"No, that was good, but the other one," she said, "and not the big one. There." Her finger found the title. "That's it. 'Losing My Mind'. More like me. My theme song."

"Tell me more of that story about the stranger in Mercy, Australia," said Robin.

"Oh yes," she said eagerly. "So the barman tells him sure they have tea, but tea not made from leaves. It's made from koala bears. Well, the stranger's disgusted, of course. But the barman says it's okay, try it, cobber, ye'll like it, it's good and hot and—" An involuntary laugh erupted out of her. She could not go on.

"Will I ever hear the end of this story?" asked Robin.

She was helpless for laughing. "I dunno," she said between gasps, "maybe not."

Both laughed.

At her door he did not try to kiss her goodnight this time. Mona Lutzky would approve, he thought, as he made his way down to his Village home.

James Bond films were a must, said Gillian, because there might be a view or two of England. And if she could see a shot of a tree from "over 'ome" she would gladly die. "I really miss the trees," she said. So that was the third date. But the moment the exciting opening sequence of the film finished and the story began, Gillian fell asleep. And snored. Robin led her out of the movie house.

He rented a car. And drove to Westport.

Feet etched prints on the cold winter sand. Trousers rolled up, he carried his shoes and socks. Gillian held her shoes and tights. Walking. Talking. The air was cold. The beach deserted. Occasionally the water nipped at their toes.

"... so, much to the surprise of the stranger, the tea is what the publican said, it's hot and good." The cold seemed to help her suppress a giggle. "But bits of fur are floating in his tea. So he takes his mug back to the barman and asks for the tea to be strained. But the barman says no, he can't do that, because — wait for it, wait for it — The Koala Tea of Mercy is not Strained." Success at finishing the story led to a sudden release of laughter. "Get it? Get it?" she asked, almost collapsing for laughing.

"Yes. Yes," he said, also laughing. "Portia. *The Merchant of Venice*. 'The quality of mercy is not strained, it falleth like the—' Is that it? Is that what I've been waiting all this time to hear? Is that your great punchline ending to—"

A high rogue wave hit the shore. Drenching them. From the waists down they stood dripping icy water.

In the lee of the boarded-up changing rooms he stripped off his shirt for her to mop up. Little use. Shivering. Cold.

Moments later they were knocking on a seaside restaurant. Though out of hours, a man, obviously the manager, opened the door, surveyed the bedraggled youngsters.

"Coupl'o' rooms upstairs," said the manager. "Take one. Use the hair dryer. Or you'll get pneumonia."

Robin arranged for dinner. And carried two large shots of whisky up the stairs.

"Don't make a mess, now," the manager shouted after them, his New England frugality catching up with his generosity, "just a towel and the dryer." He paused. "Unless o' course you want to rent the room for the night."

After a meal of hot soup and hot fish and cool wine, they were back in the car, about to leave.

"I must warn you this is our third date," he said.

"Thank God," said Gillian.

He kissed her passionately.

"Thank God for that too," said Gillian.

"Do you know what happens now?"

Gillian nodded. "Mona Lutzky tells me everything," she said.

An hour later they were in bed. Robin had to return sheepishly to face the manager and this time rent the room properly. A time of first loving. A time both would recall in years to come. He was surprised by her lack of inhibitions. She was surprised by his abilities.

"You had that many women?" she asked.

"I read books," he replied.

"Like that one by what's-'em-face, *Comfort and Joy*?"

"Dr Alex Comfort, yes," he said.

"'O tidings of Comfort and Joy'." She snuggled her naked body under the duvet. "I like my names better."

"So do I," he said.

"Y'know what?"

"What?"

"First good argument I've ever heard for literacy," she said.

He smiled. "Well, the drawings help too."

"Hmmm," she said, "prove it."

He joined her under the duvet.

Weeks later in the afterglow of the fourth occasion of making love, Gillian, her face so close to Robin's he could not focus her features into sharpness, lay staring at him for some time. And he was looking back at her, for some time. Finally she spoke.

"I love you," said Gillian.

"Ooh, that's serious," said Robin after a while, "you never said that before."

"I don't want to be hurt," she said.

"I don't want to hurt you. Ever. I love you too," he said.

An ampersand cemented them from that moment. Robin & Gillian began.

"Oh, darling, why didn't you wake me?" Gillian narrowly missed bumping her head on the hospital light above her as she sat up.

"It's all right, gave me time to think."

145

"About what?"

"About Portugal."

"I'm glad we went," she said. "Aren't you? Even with that one night in hospital." After eight days of holiday, eating more than ever, Gillian had not had a bowel movement. The consulted local doctor put her into a clinic to be 'irrigated'. "I'm a field in a farm," she had said.

"They've all been up to see me. The medical world. Knights and McDonnell and a few thousand others. New blood, they decided I needed. Gillian the vampire, that's me." She wheeled the blood bag on its mobile stand into the toilet and half-closed the door. "Oh, an' I've gained weight. Eight pounds. Good, eh? Have you been home? The boys okay? Have you eaten? More tests for me tomorrow. More tests. So they say." She was prattling on. The question of whether remission was over or not, foremost in her mind, had obviously been left unanswered.

"Been to the pub," Robin replied. "Then home. The guys send kisses. I brought your pyjamas."

"Next year China," Gillian said coming out of the bathroom, wheeling the blood in front of her. She put the pyjamas to one side. She no longer changed clothing in front of him. "We'll walk The Wall." A moment's hesitation. "Won't we?" Robin nodded. And helped her into bed. "You can go now," she said as he covered her, "I'm tired."

Robin dimmed the light and moved it to one side. "Darling, water the garden before you come tomorrow. Specially the lavatera." Robin's knowledge of flowers consisted of being able to identify tulips and roses and little else. He believed the English learned about gardens by a sort of cultural osmosis, just as he learned about canoeing on another continent. Gillian, for instance, a product of back-to-back poverty housing in inner city Birmingham, had an instinctive flair for gardening. That plus her zest for knowing meant that shortly after they moved into their house, away from flat dwellers' window-boxes to a proper garden, every available book on lawns and shrubs and flowers could be found on their shelves. She never went to the library. Books were something to cherish. Not to give back. To her it would be a betrayal to know and love a book and then return it to a public place. "Your poverty as a child is costing me a fortune," Robin once told her. In addition to buying this never-ending array of gardening books she joined the Royal Horticultural Society. Flower shows became a must. And flowers constantly filled the house. And as it was with gardening so it was with antique furniture, child psychology, cooking, clothing — she made Robin jeans and shirts — before she moved on to music and art. Still later came the courses of the Open University. A need to know was always with Gillian.

"The lavatera will be well and truly watered. Sleep well." He kissed her forehead good night.

In the car driving home Robin could not get his mind off the bouncing breasts of the holiday beaches. The dirty-old-man syndrome is starting young, he smiled to himself. Gillian had bared her breasts only once in the sun. When was it she went topless, and where? Not amongst the luxury of private swimming pools in hired villas. No, not then. But where? Spain? No, France. Years ago. The boys were toddlers. On a beach. The family was under a sun umbrella and he had looked up from his reading to see she had slipped off the bathing suit top. Nothing was said. Samuel and Michael didn't appear to notice. It lasted less than half an hour, before she covered herself again.

"At least I tried it once," she reminded Robin after the operation had removed her breast. "Once was enough."

And after the reconstruction, with her breasts enlarged, she threatened, "Hey, I got something to show now." But she never did.

Does a woman ever understand how much a man is fascinated by her breasts? Especially to the touch? Boys mark their entrance to sex by the first feel of a breast possibly more than entering a vagina. The vagina, especially to the neophyte, is a dark forbidding place into whose orifice the male being disappears. The breast is the breast. Overt, rounded, apparent and friendly. User friendly. And variable. Comes in different sizes. Sizes? Yes, m'boy. Small ones. Big ones. Two fried eggs on a frying pan chest. Egg cup fillers. Half-grapefruits. Melons. Watermelons. Coalman. Coalman? Yeah, says the fraternity house wit, if they're big enough to sling over her shoulder like bags of coal, she's a coalman. Ha, ha, ha.

The culture of the tit. The mores of the mammary gland. I was raised in a world worshipping the god Boob. Marilyn to Madonna. Films. Those black-and-white movies seen as a boy on late night television. Jane Russell and Rita Hayworth architecturally supported by superstructure brassieres. Hardening ample bosoms into a double-pronged weapon capable of piercing the chest of any male opponent. Journals. As a teenager, with the other guys from Kleber High sneaking into Grossman's drugstore for a surreptitious look at the latest *Playboy*. The centrefold girl. Gawd, look at Them! Advertising. Dreaming in my Maidenform bra. Song. It must be jelly 'cause jam don't shake like that. Newspapers. As an adult, in this country. Turn to page three. Is it Samantha? No, still, not bad. Marilyn to Madonna. And on. Hail to thee O blithe breast. Lead on, whither thou goest, I will follow. I am only a mere man. A flat-frontaged creature. Searching to fill my hands with the right pair of protruding parts. And when I find the maiden who fits the glass brassiere, she shall go to the ball, she shall leave the kitchen behind, she shall marry me, the Prince. And live happily ever after ... As long as I can fondle her tits.

149

But what to think, what to do, what to suckle, what to worship, when breasts, like the feet of gods, are also made of clay?

Robin entered the house quietly, trying hard not to wake his two sons. I must speak to them again, he thought, about breasts and vaginas and sex. Not today. Not tomorrow. But soon.

CHAPTER

17

She came out of the bathroom face scrubbed and shining, no make-up, averting eyes still red from crying, whenever possible, as she collected into a holdall those bedside and other items scattered about the tiny room. The subdued sounds of Sunday crept up from the street below. An occasional passing car, feet on pavement, water still gushing into gutters.

"*Je voudrais un taxi,*" she said into the phone, still avoiding Robin's eyes. The indistinct words of the concierge replied.

Clara was wearing dark blue shorts and top with a pattern of small flowers also blue but a lighter shade. Smart, neat, correct clothes. To his undiscerning eye it again looked like a tennis outfit although more US Open than Wimbledon. She zipped the holdall shut, put it on the trolley again where her other luggage was already stacked. A final glance about the room. And this time held Robin's eyes.

A trembling hand was extended as she came towards him. Robin decided not to take it.

"I must thank you," she said, her hand still wavering in front of her. "You're a good man," she added, "despite what—" She looked away. After a moment's silence Robin took her hand in both of his.

"I am an idiot," he said.

Her eyes returned to meet his. She brought her other hand up to his. Hands locked, they stood in the room, eyes searching from one to the other, as if to find another way of communicating.

"You helped me. I was tired," said Clara finally. A small shrug from Robin. Another pause. "Thank you," she said. And stepped back. "I'm sorry about what happened after ..." She tried to continue. "It shouldn't have. With a man and a woman in bed ... I shouldn't have come up here. I don't know why I did. I'm sorry. You are a good man." She turned away.

"I'm sorry too," said Robin aloud. Sorrier than you'll ever know, he said to himself, that it ends like this, without loving and without love. He watched her open the door.

Hearing his words of apology she tried to muster a smile at him but didn't quite succeed.

Clara manoeuvred the luggage-load out of the door. A little squeak came from the trolley's wheels. This is the way the night ends, thought Robin, not with a bang but a whimper.

She had reached the elevator and was pressing the button when Robin asked, "How do I get hold of you?" He stopped. "That is if you want me to."

"Oh!" she said sharply, seeming surprised.

From her bag Clara produced a card.

"A business card," said Robin, "can't I call you at home?"

"I'm moving soon," she said. "Work's easier."

The elevator arrived and she clanged back the caged mesh. Robin was still in the room, watching through the open door. Clara did not look back. The trolley was boarded onto the elevator. The gate shut. The elevator descended.

I will never see her again, thought Robin.

CHAPTER

18

"Well, I want to say thanks for the lovely grub," said Michael smiling at the others at the dining table, "oh and thanks for the Nintendo and the Sega and the Game Boy and the new video for our room, and – " a red splodge crept up his face " – and, and the tapes, *ET* and *The Fugitive* and ..." He was struggling to remember his many presents and where they came from. Deciding he could not say any more, he sat down quickly, lunged for his glass, and made a great show of gulping water.

The table applauded. Michael shuffled his shoulders from side to side. His face got redder. "Do we have to do this every year?" he asked.

"Yes, we do," replied Gillian firmly.

It was Samuel's turn.

Samuel rose, looking quite sophisticated in shirt, tie,

hair slicked back. He eased his chair. Lifted his glass. "To the greatest Mum in the world," he said.

Cheers, applause and cries of "Hear, hear" erupted.

"Hey, what about me?" said Robin.

"Well, since you ask, you're not bad either," said Samuel.

"Oh, thanks very much," said Robin.

Over the laughter, Samuel said, "The toast is, Mum and . . . oh yeah, Dad."

All at the table rose to drink.

Peter stayed on his feet.

"To make a Christmas dinner of such proportions is an achievement," he said. "To make a Christmas dinner of such proportions for fifteen years is a magnificent achievement. But to make such a dinner with low-fat and no-fat alternatives for me must have taxed even your culinary skills. Thank you, Gillian. Tasted the same as always. Honest. But do you think you could slip me just a tiny bit of that bacon? No? Ah, well." He raised his glass. "My toast this year is the same as always." Groans. "No, I am not one to ride on the fickle wind of change. I would like to thank—" he turned to Michael and Samuel, "Do yo think we could have some violin music here, please?" The boys obliged, humming a dirge. "I want to thank—" Peter pretended to choke with emotion and wiped away mock tears. "I want to thank the provider of this feast, without whom none of this would be possible. Ladies and gentlemen my toast is, as always, the turkey."

All rose. Michael and Samuel held up leg bones in crossed-sword fashion. Though Michael, as often before, had trouble holding the slippery bone in place. Everyone drank to the turkey.

"You know I'm no good at this sort of thing," protested Millicent. "But, yah, yah, okay, okay, I'll try." She rose. "Year after year, as Peter said, you, Gillian, and you, Robin, have given us this marvellous dinner. Me, I'd burn one stuffing let alone try to make three. We've come to take it for granted. To Peter and me and the children," she pointed to her own children seated alongside Michael and Samuel, "the holiday means coming to your house for a great nosh." Murmurs of agreement. "And I don't know what we would do if ever we had to have Christmas without—" Millicent realized where her phrasing was leading her. And stopped. Her eyes widened. "I mean, I mean ..."

Peter was soon standing at his wife's side. "What she means is," he said, "the Andersens would like to thank the Laurents for, as the children say after a party, 'for having us'." A small amount of chuckles. "It's lovely being had by you. The best havings ever had. Ever. And many more to come." He helped his wife to sit.

An embarrassed moment of silence. Gillian said nothing, turned to Robin. "You next," she said.

Robin took his time rising. "I ask you all to charge your glasses. Yeah, you two guys as well, leave the water, take some wine." His sons did so eagerly. "And rise."

He signalled Gillian not to stand. But when the others were on their feet, he said simply "To Gillian." The name echoed round the table. "Gillian. Gillian. Gillian. Gillian. Gillian ..." heard repeatedly.

"Okay, kid," said Robin sitting and turning to his wife, "spotlight's on you. Go."

Gillian, seated, started quietly.

"Thank you for being here." A murmur. "Thank me for being here." Laughter. "I like Christmas. I like the tacky cards, the useless presents, the tree, the lights, the decorations, and all the trimmings. Most of all I like this, the dinner. Turkey and cranberry sauce, parsnips, sprouts, caramelized carrots, stuffings, all those potatoes – garlic creamed, roasted, baked – mince pies and brandy butter, flaming puddings. The dullest meal of the year," she nodded towards her husband, "Robin calls it. But I like it. And he likes it because he knows I like it." She struggled to stand, leaned on the table. The claret glass in her hand reflected candlelight. "To Robin, for being the only man I married ... or ever wanted to. To Samuel for occasionally tidying up his room. To Michael who's just learning how to use the off-switch on the television. Good luck. To Peter and Millicent for being Peter and Millicent." She turned to the Andersen children. "To Vivienne who will soon know more of the answers." The plump, unattractive girl, twenty-one, shifted uneasily in her chair and looked about to make a wisecrack rejoinder but was stopped by a steady look from her father. Vivienne's older brother Mark, previously slouched to indicate his intolerance of the proceedings, now sat upright waiting for his name to be mentioned. "To Mark who already knows most of the questions." He bristled. She paused. "What is the Indian saying. God said to the world I'll give you religion. And the devil said, Yes, and I'll organize it. So today has no religious meaning to most of us. Except that it's a holiday. An excuse for families to gather. We're so stupid, we need excuses. So we gather. And look at each other. Sometimes we even see each other. The silly posturings gone. Relaxed. Drinking. Talking. Eating. And because we're crowded together, we fight. But if we're lucky we also laugh a little, as we did tonight. Laugh. And forgive. And forget. Forget the bad to make room for the good. Maybe you can't have one without the other . . . This is the loveliest country in the world when the sun is shining. We have to have the rain to make it lovely. And the bad cloudy days make us appreciate the sun more. I don't want the sunny days to end. I don't want any of the days to end." She breathed heavily. "I'm not afraid of tomorrow. Well, maybe I am, a bit. But I'd be more afraid if I didn't have today, tonight, with all of you. If you take care of today, live today, tomorrow's not nearly so frightening. Where was I? Oh yes, two sides of the same coin. Good and bad. Love and hate. Happy and hurt. I hate my cancer. But it's made me love life." She swallowed before speaking again. "It's taught me. Made me learn. You can't love life, unless you love." Another pause. "My life is you lot, here at this table." Michael started to cry. Samuel elbowed his ribs. "Christmas measures our year. Another Christmas, another year. Gone. Sad. Unless you lived the year. Lived it. Lived it ..." She sipped her wine. "We're characters in a story that began before we were born and will continue after we're gone. The Christmas story. And this dinner is part of that story. We only have so many Christmases. Only so many dinners." She raised her glass. "To life is the only toast. To celebrate the joy of being alive, and not hurt others, is the only important thing today and every day. To say thank you for the miracle of being here. That you are you and I am I. Each of us with our faults — except you, Michael, and you haven't got many either, Samuel — that we are here on this earth, in this house, at this table. Wonderful. Truly wonderful. So thank you and you and you and you and ..." She went around the table making sure she held each person's eyes as she thanked them individually, finishing on a long look to Robin. ". . . and most of all, thank you, darling." She drank the wine.

Three weeks later Gillian was dead.

CHAPTER

19

Peter and Millicent stayed on longer than expected after the Christmas dinner. Probably hoping to find the right words, now that the party was over, to make up for Millicent's faux pas at the dinner table. And to talk about Gillian's condition.

Robin had put Gillian to bed some time ago. The games were over. For the first time Gillian had not participated in charades, Trivial Pursuit, nor the card games — rummoli, racing demon, snap and sevens — she usually played with such gusto. Peter's children left soon after Gillian retired. Samuel saw Michael to bed. When Robin returned downstairs he was a little disappointed to find Peter and Millicent still firmly seated in comfortable positions.

"I helped myself, okay?" asked Peter waving a large glass filled with brandy.

"Of course."

Robin sat on the floor between them resting his back on the fireplace fender. Except for the glow from the fire and tiny lights outlining the Christmas tree, the room was in darkness. It was a setting meant for profundity so it was even more disappointing that the conversation was stilted and restricted. Peter and Millicent and Robin used up a lot of words for almost an hour. And said little. The right words were not to be found.

After the usual exchange at the door, kisses with Millicent, jokes with Peter, Robin returned to the fire. The large log was dwindling down to embers. All year Robin gathered abandoned logs on the grounds of Chiswick House and Richmond Park. He could be seen like some demented yuppie peasant struggling to manoeuvre huge pieces of sawdust-covered wood into the back of his immaculate Jaguar. Once home, the logs were stacked carefully in the garden. On Christmas morning he and his two sons would solemnly select the largest log for the fire. A family ritual. The yule log. It would be considered unlucky if the log did not last all through Christmas Day. A bad omen. A reflection on the year ahead. No such problem this year. The log still gave off abundant heat and light.

He poked the fire down. Put the mesh guard around it. Switched off the Christmas tree lights. Went upstairs.

As he softly opened the door to his bedroom, he saw Michael standing a few feet away from the bed, staring at his mother. Michael was like a statue, still, rooted to the spot, seemingly not breathing. As he came closer Robin realized Michael was crying. Large tears, disproportionate to the size of the boy's face, poured out of his eyes.

Robin signalled him to come outside.

In the hallway Michael brushed his eyes with his sleeves and the butt of his hand. "I can't stop, Daddy." He brushed again. "Make it stop, Daddy. Make it stop . . . it hurts."

Robin held his son tightly.

"It'll be all right, won't it, Daddy?"

Robin framed his son's face in his hands. "Yes, it'll be all right," he told him.

Upstairs in his bedroom, Robin found Michael's favourite part of *Jungle Book* and read to his son until the boy drifted reluctantly, sobbing, sighing with spasmodic gulps of air, into sleep.

He could hear Gillian's soft breathing as he returned to the bedroom.

"Does anyone ever realize life? Every, every minute?" Gillian had waited for Robin to settle in bed before speaking. "Isn't that the question that — what's 'er face — Emily, asks in that play, you know, *Our Town*? Does anybody ever realize life, every, every minute? And what's the answer? What does the Stage Manager reply? 'Poets and madmen, maybe.' Is that what he says? Poets and madmen."

"I think," said Robin, "it's 'Poets and saints'."
"I like my version better," said Gillian.
"So do I."
"It was a lovely Christmas," she said.
"Yes, it was."
"Goodnight, darling."
"Goodnight, Gillian."

CHAPTER

20

"Final touches to the kitchen," Gillian insisted, "still to be done." It was earlier that year; the family had been back from Portugal less than a week when decorators swarmed over the house once again. While sidestepping a paint pot on the front of the house, Gillian fell. The X-rays revealed a hairline fracture in the left hip.

The doctors refused to operate. Nor would they put her into a cast. "Let's see what time does," insisted Professor Knights. Gillian was not in pain. The morphine dosage seemed to make her oblivious of pain, and this worried Robin dreadfully, though he dared not mention it to her. Is this the beginning, he wondered, the beginning of a time where he must keep fears about her illness to himself? The separation starts. Secrets. Separate thoughts. Don't tell Gillian. The woman whom he told everything. Everything. Well, everything except about other women. Is that illicit? Is that immoral? Which is more immoral? To keep knowledge of dalliances from your wife or not to let her know her body is weakening? Is it okay to lie about extramarital fucking but not to lie about dying?

Gillian bought a series of walking sticks. For different occasions. Black. White. Designer sticks for the walking crippled. To match varying costumes. But it was a three-legged metallic monster that proved to be most useful.

One evening she stood in front of the full-length bedroom mirror, trying to decide which cane best suited her outfit. "Richard the Third!" she shouted, waving the sticks. "I could show Antony Sher how to play it." She stopped. "Ah well, at least it's more up to date than Charlie Laughton."

She looked at her mirror image for some time. If she realized she was now a mockery of her old self, which she must have done, she never showed it. The reflection that came back from the mirror was of an old-young woman, ageing with each glance, stooped, hunchbacked, skin wrinkling, holding desperately onto a stick for support. The eyes in the head were still Gillian's eyes and therefore capable of analysing her own appearance in every detail. She did not weep. Or moan. Or curse. She just stood looking at herself.

In all the time of the disease, Robin had seen Gillian break only on three occasions. Ten years ago when the Harley Street surgeon Mr Whitton had confirmed that he wanted to operate on her breast, Gillian buckled, sobbing tears over the doctor's immaculate suit. And Robin remembered feeling a moment's sliver of jealousy. How dare this stranger, this man, old man, whom Gillian met for the first time only minutes ago, be more supportive to my wife than I am? The stranger would soon change her life completely.

The second instance was the summer before her last. Samuel had spent almost three months with his Aunt Rebecca in Cape Cod. His son being fifteen, Robin felt it was time for the boy to be exposed to some of the values of his father's country. When he returned, Robin met him at the airport. On the drive into town he tried to warn his son about Gillian's deteriorating appearance. "Okay. Okay. Okay! Dad, I get it," said Samuel in the manner of teenagers to persisting fathers.

When they got to the house Samuel ran with out-stretched arms to Gillian in the kitchen. She turned. And then he saw her. His face could not help but betray his shock. His mother had changed so much. Gillian, seeing her son's face distort itself from radiant smile to fearful apprehension, broke. The tears, suppressed from the sight of others for so many years, poured out of her. After the initial hesitation, Samuel, now taller than she was, embraced his mother. He began to weep too. They stood in the centre of the kitchen, holding each other, weeping. After a while Robin put his arms around both of them, hugged them to his chest. And so the three of them formed a tableau. A silent, shaking with emotion, crying tableau.

Until young Michael came into the room and, perplexed by what he saw, said, "Hey, what's going on?" And the tableau dissolved into laughter.

The third time Robin saw Gillian cry was a year later, six days after she had made her Christmas toast. Millicent and Gillian used to alternate having dinner parties on the last day of the year. But with Gillian's illness, Millicent found herself stuck with the chore of preparing the New Year dinner for the third year running. Not that she resented it. But she approached the task with foreboding since she was openly aware that she was not the cook Gillian was. By working hard she had excelled herself to prepare a large salmon, steamed, with new potatoes, various salads and various vegetables.

In addition to the two basic families, Millicent's parents, Herbert and Antonia, were also present. Antonia unhelpfully would not leave the kitchen but shadowed her daughter's movements during the preparations without actually lifting a hand to do anything. And even more unhelpfully said things like: "Isn't she amazing? I don't know where Millie learned to cook. Certainly not from me."

Mark, Peter's son, had brought a tall, slim girl who rarely spoke and hid large bespectacled eyes as well as the rest of her face behind heaped dark ringlets but whose shyness vanished later whilst diplaying a remarkable agility when dancing. Vivienne's boyfriend was almost as plump as she was with a smile that was more gums than teeth and whose jolly, unkempt nature was restricted by a tight-fitting suit.

Samuel disappeared into the outer world immediately after dinner on the understanding that he be back — no excuses, mind — before midnight. And he was. Just. It was decreed that Michael could stay up until after Big Ben had chimed in the new year. He sat, smiling smugly, watching his elders trying to dance in a minimal space alongside a rolled rug. Herbert smoochily held Antonia close, determined to ignore the wild gyrations all around him. Robin danced with Millicent. As usual. Peter never danced. And Gillian never liked it much. So for years it had been an unwritten rule that whenever the foursome dated, Peter would sit it out with Gillian. Which he was doing tonight. Contrary to everyone's predictions, he had stopped drinking after the operation except for an occasional glass of brandy. "Have I got some bubbly for you," he winked at Gillian when she arrived, "I got Canada Dry, Perrier, Pelegrino, Highland Spring. Name it. I've got it." After the third drink, Gillian asked, "Maybe we should go mad and put some bitters in it? Or some Cassis?" Peter shouted to the dancers, "Hey, Robin, your wife is leading me astray."

Gillian, sitting in a comfortable chair in a corner, kept falling asleep for several minutes at a time. Then she would wake, startled, eyes flying wide open, looking at the others, and then smile. Peter left her side. Robin came and sat next to her, holding her hand as she drifted off to sleep again. He had had enough of dancing. To Millicent it was a way of pleasantly moving her body. To Robin dancing was a permissible prelude to sex, and since he could harbour no such thoughts in this instance, the enjoyment was reduced. He often wondered if Millicent knew how much he tolerated dancing with her rather than enjoying it.

A few minutes before midnight, the television was switched on. An argument started over which channel was best on this occasion. The traditional Scotsman in a kilt was finally agreed on.

Robin gently woke Gillian. Helped her up. As the television screen tolled out Big Ben's strokes at midnight, the group linked crossed arms to sing and dance "Auld Lang Syne". Gillian put her stick on her left arm and with Michael and Samuel on each side of her joined in the singing, her movements limited and jerky. She

170

soon gave up and stood still. Others were singing lustily. Robin freed himself from the circle of hands and moved to face his wife. Gillian's head was bowed. Michael, still holding her hand, began to stroke it repeatedly saying, "Mum, Mum," quietly. Samuel shuffled from left to right foot and back. The eyes of the others darted about the room not knowing where to settle. The dancing was dwindling to a stop. The singing faltered. Gillian raised her head. Looking steadily at Robin, she whispered, "Hold me." He did. And after a moment, he thought he could hear her murmuring, wondered what she was saying. Gillian was singing. As loudly as she could, which was not loud. Soon the others heard her too. The dancing resumed. The singing became robust again. But the only voice Robin heard was Gillian's.

> Should auld acquaintance be forgot
> And never brought to mind ...

In the car on the way back, Gillian huddled in the back, firmly gripping the arms of her two sons.

"Sorry, guys. I'll be better next year," she said.

"Of course you will," said Robin.

When they got home Robin put her to bed. And knew that Gillian knew she would never leave her bedroom again.

CHAPTER

21

Gillian never knew her mother.

"One afternoon," Gillian said to Robin, "they were all out – Grandpa, Grandma, Jeremy. Out. I went up to the loft. Found this box. Y'know the scene. Streaming sun making shafts of light. Lots of dust. And a teenage kid. Me. Coughing. In the box were papers. Legal looking papers. It was the first time I learned my mother's name. Molly. I said it to myself over and over. 'Molly. Molly. Molly. Molly . . .'"

Her mother had met an American soldier, still billeted in England despite the war's end, and had abandoned her family to return with her new love to the vastness of a new continent and the vastness of a new life. She was never heard of again.

"She must have been quite a woman," said Gillian. "Ballsy. Jeremy was a toddler – two, three years old –

and I was a babe, when she walked out. Of course, at first I hated her. How could she leave like that? And my grandparents, who raised us, and my aunts, Hilda and Beryl, especially Hilda—"

"Hilda and Beryl," interjected Robin. "When do I meet these aunts?"

"You don't," said Gillian. "I want this marriage to last." She paused. "They all made sure I hated my mother. So hate I did ... My mother was called She. That was the only reference. She. It was a topic to be avoided. Scorned. She. The scarlet woman."

"Do you want to find her?"

"No, let her find me. If she ... if Molly is still alive. Let her find me."

"What about your father?"

"He was cycling home from work, a winter night, a truck killed him. I was two. He always took me to the playground. So they say. Swings. I think I remember that. The swings and my father. But I probably created it. I was told about it so much. Be nice, though, if my visions were real. Not imagined. I have a photo of him somewhere. None of my mother."

It was a late summer night in Cape Cod. So cold that Robin had lit a log fire to warm the cabin. "I don't really need a fire," Gillian had said. But Robin insisted. Gillian was pregnant. The foetus that was to become their first-born was eight months into development.

"I've told you about this before," said Gillian, "about me ma and me pa, haven't I?"

"Not all of it."

Robin's parents were asleep in the only bedroom in the family cabin. The sisters could be heard gently snoring on the front porch. He and Gillian were to bed down in the living room, Gillian on the settee, Robin on two easy chairs pushed together.

The reminiscences had started with the lighting of the fire. She drank massive mugs of tea, he was fortified with his already habitual malt whisky. They sat wordlessly watching the flames. When she reached for a cigarette – both were smokers in those days, although during pregnancy she reduced her intake to two cigarettes after dinner – he took it from her, held it towards the fire, created suction by tapping one end until the tobacco ignited. "When I was a child, neither Jeremy nor I could put a lump – not even one lump – of coal on the fire without asking permission. I did it once and got walloped. Each lump was counted. So many to start, the minimal amount, about six usually, then more added, one at a time. When I see you throwing logs on, putting coal on with such abandon, I remember those nights. Cold nights."

"Right. No house with a fireplace for us. Is that right?" he joked.

"No, I love open fires," she said. "But I love central heating too. That's the best, real fires when you don't need real fires 'cause you have central heating."

"Then that's what you shall have."

"Your place or mine?" she asked.

"I don't mind living in your country. Don't mind at all."

"Oh, good."

"It's cold, it's damp," he said, "wages are low, costs are high—"

"It does have a National Health Service," she interrupted.

"—taxes are through the roof," he continued.

"And child benefit payments," she said.

"Tell you what," said Robin, "let's really benefit that child of ours. Let him or her be born here so that he—she can qualify for President. Then we'll go live in your place."

"President? Nah, eight years, then you're out of a job," said Gillian.

The growling voice of Robin's father interrupted. "You two gonna talk all night? Can't sleep, with you two talkin'." He stood in the bedroom doorway, wrinkled arms and spindly legs protruding from short summer pyjamas.

Robin leaped to his feet, to argue, when Gillian stopped him. "Yes, you can," she said. She held out a hand for Robin to help her up. "Stop being such a cranky old man. Grumpy." She kissed her father-in-law's cheek.

"We can't possibly be disturbing you. Whispering, we are. Go back to bed." She pecked his cheek again.

Robin's father hesitated. "You sure it's all right?" His eyes looked down at her protruding belly. "Smokin'. Drinkin'."

"Look, Dad, if we want to——" said Robin.

"He's right," said Gillian quickly. She threw the cigarette into the fire. "Now will you go to sleep. And stop being so naughty."

The old man turned in the doorway. "Sorry. Sorry. Can't sleep. Sorry, Robin. Sorry, Gillian. Sorry." He left.

Robin shook his head. "You sure know how to melt him down."

"I'm carrying his grandson," said Gillian. "And not before time. He thought he'd never live to see the day." Robin and Gillian had had difficulty conceiving. Her fallopian tubes were blocked. The irony was not lost on Robin that after years of worrying about impregnating women, he then needed help to father a child.

Robin added to his drink. "Tell me more about those exotic nights in Birmingham," he said.

"The fire was in the front parlour," she said. "Lovely, that, isn't it? 'Front Parlour.' I've seen clothes closets in this country bigger. All the other rooms had fireplaces. Unused. Fire was in that room only. So Jeremy and I would strip down to our underwear and then run like hell to jump into our beds."

"You had a bed?"

"Sure we had a bed. What do you think, we were poor or something?"

He refilled her tea mug.

"Slept side by side. Then head to toe. Then took turns on the floor." She paraphrased the song. "'Saturday Night Was the Gruesomest Night of the Week.' A tin bath. In front of the fire. A hot kettle from the stove. That was it. Until I rebelled. When womanhood approached. Grandma and Grandpa were the arbiters on everything. Led to one hell of a row. Went to the public baths after that. What luxury." She shifted her bulky body, trying to find comfort, sitting on the floor leaning against Robin's knees as he sat in an armchair. "Ooh, that's better."

"Water for the kitchen," she said. "That was it. The loo was outside at the bottom of the yard. Not what you call a yard when you mean a back garden, I mean a back of the house area touching a back of the house area of the next street. Rows of out-houses standing like sentries between fenced yards. On guard. Sentries of sanitation. Back to back. Imagine a child caught short on a sub-zero night. Wonder why I'm not permanently constipated."

"You sure you talking about this century?" he asked. "Sounds Dark Ages."

"Does, doesn't it?" she agreed.

When she was thirteen it was decreed that Gillian's education should stop. So that her brother's education could continue. Girls, ruled the grandparents, did not need to be educated. She went to work for the chocolate firm, Cadbury's. A given number of hours were to be spent at the factory school.

"At sixteen I was told my tuition and a trifle more — and a trifle it was, but I was grateful — would be paid for me to go to a polytechnic, now called collèges or universities. I read, studied to you, Art and also History of Art. I could draw."

"And Jeremy?" asked Robin.

"My brother, to use your words, flunked out of school aged seventeen. Funny, eh? I would've killed to stay at school. And he ... wasted. Wasn't till more than ten years later that he found God. Or God found him. And he became a vicar."

"More. I want more," said Robin.

"That wave, twenty years ago, of boasting about being working class — over now, thank goodness — was not for me. I wanted to get away from all that. And did." She sipped her tea. "My first night at college, in the dormitory, I was surrounded by crying girls. Away from home, hugging teddy bears, lonely, crying girls. A room of my own. A bed of my own. I didn't cry. I was in heaven." Another sip.

"Your turn," she said.

He shook his head.

"I'm saying too much," she laughed. "The 'magic' could go, the 'mystery' vanish."

They kissed. "Do me one favour. Paint more."

Many years later Gillian painted a blue-dark picture of a man cycling out of a factory gate, lunch pail in hand, bundled against the winter night, caught in the light of a lamppost. The large canvas stood proudly on the first landing of the house in West London. She called the painting: "Father, six a.m. shift".

CHAPTER

22

"It's Clara."

"Who?"

"Clara ... Clara Stromehl."

He thought he could detect an unease in her voice. "I'll have to call you back. I'm making my wife dinner." Robin had answered the phone on the kitchen hatch. In his other hand was a ladle. He kept turning from the phone to monitor the stove. Tomato soup, fresh, not tinned from Marks & Spencer, proved to be Gillian's favourite. She ate best when Robin fed her.

"How is she?" asked Clara.

"Not so good."

"Well, I thought I should call."

"Yes, thank you."

"If it's not too late, Happy New Year."

"It's never too late," replied Robin. "Happy New Year."

A bit of red soup lingered in the corner of Gillian's mouth until he gently wiped it away. A small smile from her. He smiled back. Words were rare these days. Rarer and rarer with each passing hour. Communication between them consisted of looks, nods and smiles. He spooned another load into her mouth. Waited for her to swallow. "Is everything all right, sir?" How many head waiters in how many languages all over the world had asked him and the wife he was now baby-feeding that question? In the Tour d'Argent and Taillevent in Paris, Le Pyramide in Vienne, San Pietro in Positano, Mal Maison in Los Angeles. Is everything all right, sir? Yes, fine thank you, it's just that she's dying and is having a little trouble swallowing.

"You won't be able to take care of her." Professor Knights stared unblinking at Robin as he said these words. Why don't they understand? Robin wondered. She's my wife, my woman. I can't institutionalize her, put her in a hospital, a hospice, a home. She has a home. My home. Our home. The house. I will look after her.

I can do it. I know I can't do anything else. "It'd be wonderful for her, of course, if you kept her, not so wonderful for you," said the professor, changing tactics. "She'll vomit. Become incontinent. Need nappies." The return to babydom. How Gillian would have laughed.

"Right to the end," said Robin, "she'll know where she is. And that I am with her."

Dying is the final insult. Death is the last ignominy. Waiting for all of us.

The Marie Curie nurses arrived that night. And the Ealing Council social workers and district nurses the next day. All there to help buffer the ending. To help deliver Gillian out of this world. Not that Robin wasn't thankful to them. He was.

Millicent came to see them once, sometimes twice, each day. Robin was unaware of her presence in the house one afternoon and when she came into the study he hurriedly tried to hide the book he was reading. Millicent stared at the plain-wrapped book he hadn't quite managed to get into the desk drawer.

"Porn, is it? Now? At this time?" she asked.

Like an apprehended schoolboy Robin guiltily showed her the book's contents.

"Euthanasia?" Millicent was horrified.

"I won't let her suffer. No pain. Ever," Robin said simply.

Millicent's eyes bulged out of her narrow face. "I need a cigarette," she said. "Can we go into the garden?" Once outside, the first withered rose in need of deadheading near the footpath became the object of her attentions. It would take both hands to snap the flower free. She jammed the cigarette into her mouth. Ignored the smoke curling into closing eyes. Twisted the flower off. Finally she spoke. "Y'know, Gillian and I had a long lunch here shortly after you got back from Portugal. Gillian knew that she was loved best towards the end. By you. And the boys. But especially by you. She told me she'd felt the most love she'd ever known from you. I thought you should know that." Robin nodded. "She knew about you and . . . other women. Not recently, I know, in the past. You were never as bad as Peter. But you were bad. And she always knew. But now, she is the only woman in your thoughts, she knows that." A pause. "She loved being your wife." Millicent threw her cigarette away and headed back into the house.

For the first time Robin was glad he had not made love to Clara that night in Paris.

*   *   *

"A travelling salesman goes into a brothel in the States ..." Peter was talking in the front garden of a Bayswater pub as he and Robin watched the march-past of swaying girls in summer clothes. "... and says to the Madame, 'Here's a hundred dollars, I want the worst blow job possible.' The Madame is astonished. 'But, sir,' says the Madame, 'for a hundred dollars I can get you the best blow job possible.' 'I know,' says the salesman, 'but I'm homesick.'"

It was a hot July night. Gillian and Millicent were at the Royal Opera House seeing Placido Domingo as Otello. Girls' night out. Baby sitters guarded the children. The boys were having a night off too.

"I can rely on you, can't I, not to tell Millicent? About Caroline?" asked Peter. He had spent most of the afternoon with a plump, buxom brunette who had joined the agency as a junior executive the week before. The two men were still unsure of each other. Their partnership was not yet two years old.

"Hate to disappoint you," replied Robin, "but you can be absolutely certain I will never tell Millicent."

"Pardon?" said Peter.

"You want her to know," said Robin. "Notches on your gun."

"Oooh. Sounds painful." A large gulp of brandy swirled into Peter's mouth.

The two men had been drinking for some time.

"Haven't you ever ... strayed?" asked Peter.

Don't you know about Louise? Louise Borden? The lady from Hexler Foods Inc. Condensed milk. Baked beans. Corn on the cob. Corny. Say that again. Corny. In tins ... Good time to tell you about Louise. Boys' night out. Confessing. Bragging. There's this girl Louise ... No, don't mention Louise. Not to Peter. Or anyone. Ever.

"I think it's time to wrap," said Robin.

Peter waved the suggestion aside. "Oh, Millicent knows all about me, me and my, my wanderings. We talk about it."

"Do me a favour," said Robin, "do yourself a favour, and above all do Millicent a favour. Don't. Don't talk about it." He rose from the table. "G'night, pardner. Ah'm gonna sashay on home."

He left Peter sitting in the pub.

CHAPTER

2 3

Samuel and Michael took to doing their homework in the master bedroom. Nothing was said. Samuel was first, clearing a space at Gillian's dressing table. Michael followed, sitting cross-legged on the floor, his books in front of him, under a lamp.

So Gillian would wake after long periods of sleep to find the three males in her life around her.

Her sleep lasted for hours. Her wakefulness for moments only. Sometimes she managed a word. "Maths?" she said to Michael one evening, seeing her son frowning at the foot of her bed.

Michael nodded, "How did you know, Mum?"

Gillian laughed her laugh out loud for the first time in ages. The others laughed too. Then she fell asleep with a small smile on her face.

Robin started to bring the evening meal upstairs. With

Samuel's help. A trayload each would be transported onto a chest converted into a makeshift dining table. With cushion piles for chairs. But at least it meant they were near her. Conversation was subdued. The boys would find a topic, or start an argument, in order to pretend not to notice the mess being made as Robin struggled to feed their mother.

Until the night nurse arrived to shoo them out of the room. "Well, I guess I'll go tidy up my room, Mum," said Samuel. Another laugh from Gillian. She tried to speak. Realized she couldn't. Laughed some more. Closed her eyes.

The trio lined up to kiss her goodnight.

With the arrival of the nurses Robin was banished from sleeping beside Gillian.

Those whom God hath joined together were put asunder not by man but an efficient nurse. The marital bed looked more and more like a hospital bed. Tubes and tubs, bedpans and commodes, pills and potions, replaced bedside ornaments. Robin's feelings were mixed. He needed to rest more, to sleep. But he wanted to be alongside Gillian as much as possible.

He slept in the guest room, across the hall, handy if needed but sufficiently apart. He had lost weight, of course. Eating less and less. Awake too many hours.

He did not go to work. The office avoided calling him, managing to maintain silence for about forty-eight hours on average before some emergency — though he thought it always trivial — summoned him to the phone. He suggested the best time to reach him was between eleven and midnight. So he would lie in bed, a phone near his head but all others unplugged, and wait. And think. And remember. And dream.

That July night in Paris would come flooding through his brain. The restaurant, her pyjamas, in bed with his hand on her hip, the white look of her at the airport, the tassels of her sweater bobbing on her back, the taxi ride, her nakedness, breasts rising and falling, nipples, all etched itself into his mind, repeating the most minute details in no particular linear order, jumping about in time as one memory segued to another.

Always ending up at the same question: Why hadn't he made love to Clara?

Reasons arrayed themselves in his mind to form a list for checking.

It was some hormonal imbalance that had reduced his masculine aggression. Maybe it happens to a man whose body has not been loved for two years . . .

Or maybe it just happens with age. Was he too old for

her? Yes, probably. That's why he didn't do it! Definitely! Is it . . . ?

He liked her too much. He couldn't have fallen in love with her in the few hours they were together, but he had grown to like her, to respect her. And that's bad. Respect can kill any fornication . . .

For Clara read Louise. Louise Borden. Louise of Hexler Foods Inc. The can company. He had met Louise twelve years earlier. In Argentina. She was from New York, the Hexler representative on a big shoot that went wrong. That meant a reshoot. More than once. Altogether he was away from London, except for the occasional weekend, for over four months. An apartment forty miles west of Buenos Aires became home. And Louise was there. When not in Argentina he was in New York. And Louise was there. He fell in love with Louise. But could never countenance leaving Gillian and the children. Louise said she understood. For the next three years they loved each other episodically in Wisconsin or Goa, Montreal or Aberdeen, and even, London or New York. Then the meetings became less and less frequent. Until it dwindled to just lunches. Or teas at Claridge's. Or phone calls. Come to think of it, Clara looked like Louise. Same almost-blonde hair, fluorescent white skin, eyes. That's what he was looking for. He didn't want to spoil what could be a longer relationship by having a one-night stand. He wanted another Louise. So he controlled himself . . .

It is wrong, morally wrong, to take advantage of a

woman on her own. Oh c'mon, Robin, maybe the woman wanted you to take advantage of her? And it was morally wrong of you not to take advantage! Oh my God . . . !

Paris can be lonely. Any place can be lonely. She was good company. He was grateful. That was enough . . .

Rape. He was afraid she might scream rape. A woman he didn't know. In a hotel bedroom. It was a chance he couldn't take . . .

He behaved to her as he would want a man to behave to him if he were a woman . . .

Maybe deep in his psyche he felt responsible for Gillian being ill. It was his fault. He destroyed women. Like a perverse Midas turning everything he touches to disease. Ergo he wouldn't touch Clara . . .

Myth and reality. Which was which? The yearning for a beautiful woman beside him, in bed, in a hotel room, in Paris of all places. That was so much what he wanted. And it came true. The myth had become real. It would shatter like glass if handled badly . . .

Guilt. He could make love. Gillian was lying in another bed. Crippled . . .

Perhaps, for all our faults as a species, we have certain pleasant attributes as well. Kindness is one of them . . .

He just couldn't be bothered. Considering what was happening in his life at the time, the last thing he wanted was to be covered in a morass of emotions from which he could not escape. He didn't make love to Clara that night because he didn't want to make love. It was as simple as that. He couldn't be bothered . . .

Nothing happened because nothing was meant to happen. Given that mix, those two people, Clara and Robin, and who they were and what they were, nothing was meant to happen . . .

Each night Robin added another theory, another reason, as to why he had not made love to the girl from San Diego. Always finishing on the same conclusion: no conclusion was possible . . .

That didn't stop his imagination from picturing what he should have done. Entering her. Parting the vulva. Rocking back and forth. Thrusting in and out. The pictures had inspired his masturbation many times since that night. He was debating whether or not to masturbate when the phone rang.

"Sorry, Mr Laurent," said the voice, "it's about the Marston shoot which we prep tomorrow . . ." Robin was grateful for the interruption.

*　　*　　*

Aunts Hilda and Beryl arriving at Logan airport were easy for Robin to identify. Two ladies in floral straw hats and not quite complementary cotton frocks, attire more suitable for a country church than a transatlantic flight, stood out from the other passengers descending from the aircraft. Hands to brows to shield eyes from the Boston sun, the aunts squinted at the barriered crowd. Robin waved. After hesitating, the twosome waved back, before being hustled off towards the terminal building.

"Hilda's the plump one," Gillian had said, "and does the talking."

His sisters Rebecca and Ruth were with Gillian at the cabin. Robin's father and mother had come along to form a committee to receive the two maiden aunts from England.

"This is my wife Katherine," said Robin Senior, smoothly making the introductions.

"How nice," said Aunt Hilda.

"How nice," said Aunt Beryl.

A lot of kissing took place. Robin joined in, kissing his new relations European style, on both cheeks.

"Ooh, Robin, how nice," said Aunt Hilda, "nice to meet'cha."

"Yass, nice to meet'cha," echoed Aunt Beryl.

"But where's Gillian?" asked Hilda.

"Baby's due any second," Robin explained. "We didn't think it wise. It's a bit far."

Aunt Hilda's lips tightened. "Yass. Not wise. I see. I see."

"I see," also said Aunt Beryl.

"Can't tell y' how pleased we are y' could come," said Robin's father. He held out two bunches of flowers. "Fresh this morning, from around the cabin," he said. "Won't last long, I'm afraid. Wild flowers."

"How nice," said Aunt Hilda. Robin noted that whenever Aunt Hilda said 'nice' it sounded more like 'nay-ce'. "How nice." She looked at the flowers. "Pink and blue, my favourite colours. Gillie must've told you. She didn't? Ah well. Wise of her not to come all this way. As you said. Yass. Wise of her. But then she always was, wise I mean, expect you know that, Robin. How thoughtful of you to leave her at home. How nice."

On the long drive back to Cape Cod conversation gushed in spurts.

"Is there anythin' special you want to do tonight?" asked Robin's father.

"Please don't go to any trouble," said Aunt Hilda. "Just a bite. And then to bed."

"All arranged," said father.

"How nice," said Aunt Hilda.

During a pause in the conversation Aunt Hilda issued whispered instructions to Aunt Beryl.

"Ah, bu-ut they're loovely," Aunt Beryl protested. Her sister wanted to chuck the wild flowers out of the car.

"Stickin' in me," explained a sweetly smiling Aunt Hilda. "And, as you said, be dead soon. D'youse mind?"

Robin's father's face became a mask. "O' course not," he replied.

"How was the flight?" asked Robin.

"I didn' know drink were free on airplane. How can anyone be afraid of flying? Eh, Beryl?" asked Aunt Hilda.

Beryl nodded and giggled then nodded and giggled some more.

Robin's father was having difficulty with the squashed vowels of Hilda's top-speed Midland accent. He became more and more irritable. Until eventually he abandoned trying to comprehend all that was being said. But, as with many a stranger in a foreign land, would seize on any word he understood and try to formulate sentences accordingly. How gallant of you, Dad, thought Robin. Age is mellowing even you. Struggling to make chitchat. In order to make visitors more welcome.

"I think Dad was expecting cut-glass enunciations," Robin told Gillian that evening. "Oxford or Cambridge. David Niven or Cary Grant. What he got was Daffy Duck. From Birmingham, England."

"When we said cabin I don't think me dear aunts realized we meant cabin. I think they were expecting a Waldorf in the sticks," said Gillian. "Dinner is going to be a disaster. Can't wait."

It had been hoped the two aunts would manage to get

some sleep before dining. But when Robin knocked at the door of the bedroom, vacated for them, they were finishing off a duty-free bottle of Cointreau.

At the dinner table Beryl, head supported by two mean little fists, allowed her eyes to close too often. Hilda began to pontificate.

"Babies should be born at home," she proclaimed. "I don't trust hospitals."

Gillian asked lightly, "You any good at epidurals, Aunt Hilda?"

It had been Robin Senior's idea to invite the two aunts over for the birth. "Some of her family should be present." Gillian said it wasn't necessary. But the father insisted. Gillian, by now more than capable of holding her own with the old man, eventually capitulated.

Her grandparents were long dead. Her brother Jeremy and his wife Vanessa could not make the trip on such short notice. "God keeps me busy," proclaimed Jeremy on the transatlantic phone. Aunts Hilda and Beryl were sent for.

"You'll be sorry," Gillian said.

The aunts ate little of the roast beef Robin's mother had prepared so carefully that night. "How nice," said Aunt Hilda dutifully. She rubbed a linen napkin across her mouth several times. "Is there a drop more?" she asked, shoving her glass forward. The question brought Aunt Beryl back to consciousness and, smiling, she too pushed her glass towards the head of the household.

"I'll get it, Dad," said Robin, rising from the table to fetch more wine. Three bottles had been consumed. Since the hosts — Robin, his parents, sisters, and Gillian — were barely drinking, the abilities of the Birmingham ladies were all the more notable.

"What are you calling the baby?" asked Aunt Hilda when her wine glass had been refilled.

"If it's a girl," said Gillian, "Molly."

The wine glass stopped at Aunt Hilda's mouth. But only for a moment. She gave Gillian a hard look. Gillian smiled back. "My mother's name," said Gillian. Aunt Hilda resumed drinking.

"If it's a boy I'd like it if y' followed tradition," said Robin's father, "and called him Robin."

"If it's a boy," said Gillian, "his name will be Samuel."

"Oh?" The old man was disappointed. "Was that the name of your dad?"

"No," said Gillian, "I just like the name."

Under the table Robin squeezed his wife's hand.

The aunts were not interested in seeing the glories of Cape Cod. Two or three attempts the next day to entice them to visit freshwater lagoons or beaches or even Hyannisport, failed. "How nice," was all Aunt Hilda said when she finally appeared on the porch and stared down to the sea. Aunt Beryl said nothing. Both couldn't wait to get back to the bedroom and firmly shut the door behind them.

Baked ducks were presented for dinner that night.

Aunt Hilda picked at a bit of the crispy skin. "How nice," she said. Wiped her mouth. Ate no more. But drank continuously.

"Is there an off-licence nearby?" asked Aunt Hilda on the third day.

"She means a liquor store," explained Gillian.

"It's a drive," said Robin.

"Ooh, I like a drive," said Aunt Hilda. "Did I give the 'mpression I don't like a drive? We both like a drive. If there's a reason. Will you take us? How nice."

In a supermarket in Provincetown, Aunt Hilda, declining the use of basket or trolley, struggled to the checkout counter, her arms loaded with two bottles of green Chartreuse, two bottles of yellow Chartreuse and a bottle of Benedictine. One bottle slipped. And crashed. Robin offered to pay. The management refused. Aunt Hilda stared mesmerized as the spillage was mopped up by a young assistant. She seemed to be giving serious consideration to falling on her knees and lapping up the precious liquid. Aunt Beryl giggled.

In the car on the way home no conversation of any kind took place between the trio of shoppers.

That night at dinner Robin's mother once again provided an elaborate meal. Lamb stew, served in a huge tureen. Aunt Beryl appeared to be asleep, her elbows straddling an untouched plate. Aunt Hilda, after allowing the minutest amount of food to enter her mouth, said, "How nice." Whereupon Robin's mother stood up.

"Have some more," she said, "And more! And more! More! More!" From the tureen she vehemently slopped out ladlesful of stew onto Aunt Hilda's bowl. The food splattered across the table. Aunt Hilda was soon polka dotted with bits of lamb and carrots and peas and onion.

"Katherine!" said Robin Senior. "Woman, what's got into y'? Have y'gone—?"

His wife glared back at him. "It took me three hours to make dinner," she said. "Three hours! Gillian's not eating 'cause she's upset. Robin's not eating 'cause Gillian's not eating. And if you," she turned to Hilda, "say 'How nice' to me once more I'll – I'll—" She slammed the tureen down in the centre of the table and left the room in tears.

Silence.

Gillian began to applaud. "Bravo!" she said. "About bloody time!" And exited to find her mother-in-law.

The next morning at Logan airport, Robin and his father watched the two aunts board the aircraft. Aunt Hilda was talking. Aunt Beryl was giggling. Neither of them looked back as the steps were mounted.

"Let's go home and have a drink," said Robin's father.

"If there's any left," said Robin.

Father and son drove back to the cabin unaware that Gillian was giving birth to Samuel at that moment.

"I wanted to be here," said Robin to Gillian at the hospital.

"Next time," she said, "next time a picnic without aunts."

CHAPTER

24

Dying is not a tranquil time. Death does not necessarily come in stealth. Or alone. Death has accomplices. Cohorts. The soft whispering of "Rosebud" from the moustache-grey mouth as the glass of life falls from the hand. A gentle concept. So is the declamation, "The rest is silence". Well, not here it ain't, dear Prince of Denmark, not in Bedford Park, West London. Here dying is a busy business. Visitors. Friends. Neighbours. Then friends of friends. Neighbours of neighbours. Parents from the school run. Parents of Michael's friends. Parents of Samuel's friends. "Just checking, anything we can do? Anything. You will let us know, won't you?" Shopkeepers. "Lilies of the valley, first of the season, for your wife." Yes, thank you, Mr Patel. Annie, from across the road, volunteers to go to Marks. No, thank you, Annie, really no. Millicent offers to cook dinners. No, thank you, Millicent, no. No outsiders. Not now. The animals, one of them wounded, have retreated to their lair. And still they come. Strangers. Knocking at the door. Come in. Come in. Doctors. Night nurses. Day nurses. Rota nurses. Nurses. Social workers. Health workers. Therapists. Fill in this form. Just a few questions. Deliveries. Voices on the intercom. "Council delivery, a commode." "Council delivery, bedpan." "Council delivery, rubber sheets." Followed by a simple "Council delivery" as a silent driver hands over a large packet of unnamed diapers. And phone calls. From around the corner or over an ocean. From Vanessa in Newcastle. From Rebecca in New Jersey. "Shall I come over? If you want me to, I'll come over." Post. Cards and letters by the score. Shopping. Food for the boys. Tea for the nurses. "Buy some dry shampoo." Dry shampoo? "Yes, the chemist will know." "Your wife would want her hair done, wouldn't she, sir?" Yes, yes, she'd be very particular about how she looked. Wouldn't want to leave with the wrong impression. "Get this prescription filled, prohibited drug, your wife needs it. The chemist will know." Change the bed, often. Change the bed linen, often. Washing. Laundry. Cooking. Cleaning.

And find time to talk to Gillian. Talk. Speak. Say something. And neither wait for nor expect an answer. But know she hears you. Gillian is listening.

Dying is not a tranquil time. Death crowds a day. Dying is a busy business.

CHAPTER

25

In the last days, when Gillian could no longer swallow, a motorized syringe was fitted to her chest to inject morphine at intervals. The pills had long since been replaced by medication in liquid form. Then followed the morphine syringe. Robin would also swab small amounts of water onto her tongue. "Keep her mouth moist," he was told. Once, when she appeared uncomfortable, he shook her and shouted, "Gillian, Gillian! Are you in pain?" She opened her eyes briefly and said, "No", as if puzzled by the question. And returned to sleep.

On the last morning, Mrs McGilroy, the best of the night nurses, met him at the bedroom door. The pattern of Gillian's breathing had changed to short, raspy rhythmic sounds.

"I have to go," said Mrs McGilroy. "It's me this morning. The school run. My daughter's waiting. Some geography test this morning. But," she nodded towards Gillian, "she'll be all right. Get some water into her, if you can."

Robin quickly saw the nurse out. By the time he returned, Gillian's breaths were long and silent. He had to put his head near her chest to hear any sound. He could see her breasts clearly, the healthy right breast, the replaced left breast, rising and falling slowly as life ebbed away. He pulled the nightdress higher, to shield even husbanding eyes from her breasts. Her breasts. The source of all this anguish.

Robin kept his face close to Gillian. He kissed her cheek. No response. He stared. He willed her to open her eyes. His body tense. His brain hurting with concentration. Please, please, just once more, look at me. After a long time, she did. Gillian's eyes opened. His face, so close, must have filled her sights. Husband and wife, faces hardly apart, saw each other.

She attempted a smile. "Robin." It was the last word she said. Her eyes closed.

CHAPTER

2 6

For richer, for poorer
In sickness and in health . . .

The ceremony was a simple, short affair in front of
a justice of the peace who distinguished himself in
Robin's memory by being unable to take his eyes off
Gillian. "Your bride is beautiful," whispered the justice
as Robin leaned forward to sign the register. Robin
looked at him. A middle-aged man, medium height,
medium weight, medium everything; a few loose hairs
straggling across a balding pate, wearing a shirt collar
too small for a tie too tight, under a suit of indeterminate
stripes. Sweating. Smiling. A middling man. Who had
the power, and minutes earlier had exercised it, to
grant society's approval on this man's and this woman's
decision to share life. Robin followed the justice's gaze.

Gillian stood kissing and being kissed, congratulated by the few guests, mainly Robin's family, plus one friend from the office. What was the friend's name? Oh yes, Mary. Mary Whatling. Whatever happened to Mary Whatling? Gillian's flatmate, Sally Anne Willens, for some reason, never made it to the wedding. But Mona Lutzky, head of the typing pool, and famous for making sure all the girls knew everything, did. Robin looked again at the justice to ensure that his remark was not a sneer or a leer or a nudge-nudge comment. It wasn't. It was just a grin.

"Ye wouldn't do it in a church." His father cornered him. "We could've had the whole town out. Instead of this." His thin patrician face was even thinner with anger. "My son married. Married without God."

"Well, I didn't want to bother Him," said Robin.

The old man glared at him. Robin and Gillian had given less than a day's notice that they intended to wed.

"No consideration for—" said his father.

"You going to hit him on the head for disobeying?" interrupted Gillian.

Robin's father stared at his new daughter blankly, oblivious of the reference to childhood punishments meted out to his son.

"Dad," Robin spoke gently, "it's our wedding. This is what we wanted."

His father nodded. "I'm sorry," he said. "I ..."

He lifted his arms and for a moment it appeared he would embrace his son. Robin waited. But all the father managed was to brush a hand against his son's shoulder. Before he walked away.

"No one's going to hit your head now," said Gillian.

Robin laughed. "Only me," he said. "I may bang it against a few windmills from time to time.

"I sincerely hope so," said Gillian.

His sisters Rebecca and Ruth were signalling for help with a distressed mother who was seated in a chair, tears pouring onto her cheeks, taking big gulps of air to compensate for not being able to breathe normally. "Oh, Robin, Gillian," she said, hiccuping and gulping in discomfort, "I'm so happy for you, so happy."

"Yes, I can see that," said Robin. His mother laughed. And clearly determined to hide her weeping, buried her face by embracing them both.

Mona Lutzky was also crying. "I can't help it, I can't help it," she kept repeating. Robin found a chair for Mona and inadvertently placed it opposite his mother. So the two weeping women sat facing each other. Realized they were creating a sight, they tried hard not to catch each other's eye. But did. And laughed. And cried. And wailed even more.

"Corny," said Gillian, looking at the tearful twosome, "isn't it corny?" Robin smiled. "It's a cliché. And I hate clichés, you know that. I loathe clichés." He nodded. "For instance, there's 'You made me the happiest woman in the world' and 'Today is the happiest day of my life.' Yuk."

He looked at the woman who was now bonded to him.

"There's another cliché," he said. "It goes, 'I love you.'" They kissed.

The kiss was curative. Mona stopped crying. Mother started to breathe regularly. Robin found himself in front of his father. For a long time he looked deep into the grey-blue eyes of the older man. "Dad," he said suddenly and hugged his father to his chest. He kissed a white stubble of beard.

"Robin," said his father, "Robin . . ."

His son held him tight. "I know, Dad, I know . . . It's okay. It's okay."

A piercing screech from Mona Lutzky. Never one to speak softly, the excitement raised her voice to even more decibels. "Oh m'gawd! Oh m'gawd!" she said. "There's only one shot left!" Mona was the only person with the presence of mind to have brought a camera. She had busied herself earlier taking pictures of all those present. Except the bride and groom.

Robin told her not to bother. "No! No!" she said. "Gotta have something of you two. For your kids. For us. For me. Somebody run to the drugstore. Here's money. Get me some more film. Oh gawd, there won't be time! Wait! Wait! Don't go yet!" She pointed an old Brownie at the newlyweds. "No," she ordered, "y'can't stand there. That window's awful! No, not by that wall! That's a real mumzer of a wall! Where? Where? Oh! I know."

Mona manhandled the couple outside. The exterior doorway leading to Provincetown court rooms with an arched canopy overhead was, she decided, the only suitable place. She asked the bride and groom to compose themselves while she ran down the steps in front of them. "Keep everybody back. Just these two. Sorry, sir, y're probably from the Supreme Court," she shouted to a well-dressed interloper, "and y'll send me to jail forever, but d'y'mind?" The man cowered away. "Ready?" Her voice foghorned obedience, keeping any more would-be intruders from the area. "Okay?" she demanded. "Now!" Snap.

Mona beamed happily. The prized photo was in her camera. She ran back up the steps to Gillian and Robin. "About tonight," she asked, "shall I tell you everything . . . ?"

"I don't think so," said Gillian, embracing her, "not everything."

"Well, I'd like to know," Robin countered. "Maybe you should tell me. Everything!"

Laughter. The family and guests came out on the steps to add their goodbyes to the departing couple.

Years later the wedding photograph would be taken out from a drawerful of other such souvenirs. And marvelled at. In the world of photography it would not win awards. The two principals were framed awkwardly off to one side. There was more door and archway showing than there was bride and groom. Neither Robin nor Gillian looked their best. But still . . . How young she was. How slim. How innocent. The small smile on her face betraying some anxiety as well as hope. And you, Mr Justice of Peace, you were right. She was beautiful. And oh, how happy. How happy . . . How happy . . . How alive . . .

Robin found himself staring at a dying Gillian.

CHAPTER

27

Dr Lundt, the family physician, had warned him the final breathing sounds made a rattling noise and were not pleasant to hear. He was right. Robin waited for the sounds to stop before he roused his sons.

"Mum is leaving us," he said gently to Samuel. His firstborn left the bed quickly. Michael was always more difficult to waken. "Wha . . . ? What is it?" he asked. Robin repeated the same phrase, "Mum is leaving us. Come."

Robin stood, holding the hand of a son at either side of him, at the foot of Gillian's bed. Silently the trio watched. And waited. Michael finally pulled away. Ran to his mother. And covered her face with kisses. Endlessly kissing, he tried to speak, but failed. His wet face, begging for help, looked up at his father and brother. Samuel shuffled closer, took his mother's hand, then let it drop.

The boys moved back to their father. Faces buried, leaned on Robin. He held them tight as they wept.

It was over.

Husband. The tiller of the soil. The provider. The protector. Even unto death. Nay, especially unto death. Protect. Shield. When the wife is dying, justify your reason for casting a shadow on this planet, care for her to the end, to the oh so bitter end. Justify your marriage. Be a helpmate. A guardian. Be a husband.

To be a husband one needs a wife.

CHAPTER

2 8

"My wife died last week." How eerie it was to hear himself say that. "The funeral was yesterday." He paused. "I don't know why I called."

"I'm glad you did," said Clara.

"Well, maybe I'll call again," said Robin. "Or you call me. I'm sorry. I . . ."

He hung up.

The house was empty. The noise and bustle of yesterday's mourners now silenced. Samuel and Michael were with Aunt Vanessa in Newcastle for a few days. And would return to school next week. Robin was alone.

The house that Gillian had filled merely with her presence, mourned her absence by seeming quieter than ever. Too quiet. It's not right for a house to be this quiet. But he could not bring himself to move or make a sound. He remained where he was. Silent. Wordless. Still. Quiet.

✳   ✳   ✳

"Are you sure, sir?" asked the funeral director.

What was Gillian doing in a funeral parlour? Such places are for other people. For dead people. Talking to funeral directors, making burial arrangements, that's for others, Gillian, not for us.

"Yes, I'm sure," Robin replied.

It was the morning of her funeral. The undertaker, whose name Robin would never remember, removed the coffin lid. It had not been sealed, it was explained, in case relatives or friends wanted 'a final glimpse of the deceased'. None did. Only Robin. The lifeless body looked more a replica of Gillian than Gillian herself. Still he was tempted, Laertes-like, to take her in his arms once more. One final time. One last embrace.

"And the ring, sir," said the undertaker, "you still want it left?"

Robin insisted that Gillian was to be cremated wearing her wedding ring. "She would have wanted that," he said simply. A slight sigh of disapproval from the undertaker. The lid was about to be replaced.

"Just a minute," said Robin. From his breast pocket he produced a wrapped Crunchie. Gillian's favourite chocolate bar. "To make your journey sweet, my darling," he said. He put the bar in her hand. And nodded to the undertaker. Who was too bewildered even to sigh. The lid was sealed.

❊   ❊   ❊

"God hates funerals," said the vicar, "that's why it's always so cold." It was a clear sunny day with a biting February wind. The courtyard in front of the crematorium was filled with people. And flowers. Flowers and flowers and flowers and flowers.

Earlier the cortege had come to collect Robin and his two sons. Then, in customary English fashion, the funeral director had walked bareheaded in front of the hearse from the house — the house she cherished so much — as far as the end of the road. The procession passed the green where Gillian had taken her babies to toddle and run and skate and cycle, passed the parade of shops where Gillian had been a prime patron. Post office and butcher and greengrocer and fishmonger and numerous boutiques. Landmarks for the living. Oblivious of the sad caravan passing by. "It's right that we should come this way," whispered Samuel. Robin agreed. He sat between his boys in the back of a black limousine following the coffin-carrying glass-sided wagon.

Peter and Millicent were waiting at the courtyard. And other friends. And neighbours. People from his office. And Dr Lundt. And the dentist. The lawyer. The butcher, the baker, the candlestick maker, they're all here. Robin appeared to know everyone but spoke only briefly to a few for he was too concerned for his sons to pay too much attention.

A woman approached him who looked only vaguely familiar. Who is she? He felt he should recognize facial features enlarged by age. But he couldn't place her.

"Robin, you don't remember me," she said. "I came over when I heard. I'm Mona Lutzky."

Robin broke. His sons had to lead him into the chapel.

Life is a story without a happy ending.

CHAPTER

29

"We all think y're dead." Robin was saying it to Gillian. An alive Gillian. Not only alive but healthy. The Gillian of years ago. Sparkling. She did not answer but managed to convey her regret at being mischievous and causing such trouble. She laughed. He could see her laugh. And yes, yes, if he strained, he could even hear her laugh. That laugh! That laugh! Then a wave goodbye. A final look back over her shoulder. Gillian. Happy. Radiant. Smiling. And she was gone.

A dream. A wish. A vision he had been having by night and sometimes by day during the many nights and days since her death. What brought it on now? The whisky-sodas? Hurtling through space thousands of feet above the planet? Don't go, please Gillian, don't go! He tried to force the vision of her back into his head.

"Can I get you another drink, sir?" asked the stewardess.

Robin shook his head. He closed his eyes. Concentrated. But Gillian would not return.

He was on an airplane. Hallucinating, dreaming, longing for his wife. It was more than a year since Gillian had died. A long year. A year with every day measurable. A year of long days. And not one day had passed in that year of long days without his thinking about Gillian. Mourning her, weeping, howling, yes, screaming howls to pierce the night. Or just sitting still, numb with yearning. Not a day that he did not think of her. Ah Gillian, Gillian. My lover, my woman, my wife. I miss you. I miss you. I miss you. My lover. My woman. My wife.

A tear escaped from below his lashes. He wondered, am I crying for Gillian? Or is it like all tears, only for oneself? He looked out of the window. Lifted the dregs of the whisky and soda to his lips.

"Forgive me, Gillian," he said almost aloud.

Will I be able to love Clara? It's easier to be unfaithful to a living wife than to a dead one. I will never get over Gillian. Never. Ever. But Gillian is gone. Clara is life.

Clara said she would be at the airport to meet him.

Warner Books now offers an exciting range of quality titles by both established and new authors. All of the books in this series are available from:

Little, Brown and Company (UK),
P.O. Box 11,
Falmouth,
Cornwall TR10 9EN.

Alternatively you may fax your order to the above address. Fax No. 01326 317444.

Payments can be made as follows: cheque, postal order (payable to Little, Brown and Company) or by credit cards, Visa/Access. Do not send cash or currency. UK customers and B.F.P.O.: please send a cheque or postal order (no currency) and allow £1.00 for postage and packing for the first book, plus 50p for the second book, plus 30p for each additional book up to a maximum charge of £3.00 (7 books plus).

Overseas customers including Ireland please allow £2.00 for postage and packing for the first book, plus £1.00 for the second book, plus 50p for each additional book.

NAME (Block Letters) ....

....

ADDRESS ....

....

....

☐ I enclose my remittance for ....

☐ I wish to pay by Access/Visa Card

Number ☐☐☐☐☐☐☐☐☐☐☐☐☐☐☐☐

Card Expiry Date ☐☐☐☐